The Fake Birthday

by
Gerri Rudner & Suzan Jaffe

ISBN: 1-4392-0150-1

ISBN-13: 9781439201503

Visit www.booksurge.com to order additional copies.
Author contacts: szscribbles@yahoo.com and
rremgt@verizon.net

The Fake Birthday

CHAPTER 1
OBSESSIONS

 Today's Horoscope:

Scorpio (October 24-November 22): A dream will be fulfilled today. Go for broke. Past obstacles will no longer prevent you from reaching your goals. Tonight: accept an invitation.

I can't remember how it started, but I truly, truly believe in horoscopes. Maybe it happened when my mom, Sharon Milner, was pregnant. She told me that I kicked her for the first time when she was reading her daily horoscope. Could it be that my parents met under a full moon? Or my annoying older sister, Becky, may have thrown a fake stuffed scorpion into my crib while I was sleeping. It could also have something to do with my crazy Aunt Tillie wearing her purple wig and star-covered cape when she came to visit us one Halloween. She let me try it on, and I remember loving the way the velvet felt against my skin...so soft and smooth, even though it stunk from the gallons of this smelly perfume she's been wearing since forever. Anyway, I could give you a trillion reasons why I'm a zodiac queen. I was born under the sign of Scorpio. Whatever. I just plain love the stars, and never get bored of figuring out what they have to say to us mortals. I mean real live people, not galaxy gods.

So, every morning I turn to the last page of the magazine section of the *Forrester Tribune* and read my horoscope.

I would love to cut it out of the paper, but my dad, Dr. Barry Milner, would go ballistic because it would destroy the crossword puzzle on the other side. Dad does the puzzle every night because he says it helps him fall asleep. It's part of his bedtime obsession. I still don't get it. How can figuring out a clue like "eight-letter word for the TV show _____ *Idol*" knock him out for the night? I mean, really?

And that's just the beginning of my dad's ridiculous nightly routine. It's pretty funny, the way he fluffs up four down pillows and positions them carefully against the headboard. Then, he unwraps a stick of Puckers wintergreen chewing gum, rolls the wrapper into a tiny ball, and shoots it across the bedroom toward the wastebasket. Because he only chews each stick until the flavor runs out, he can go through two to three packs of gum before turning off the light to go to sleep. Do you want to hear something hilarious? Guess what Dad does for a living? He's a dentist; a gum-chewing dentist. Do you really think a dentist should be chewing so much gum?

Just this morning, as my mother bent over to pick up all those tiny little wrapper balls that never scored points, she yelled, "That's it! It's bad enough that my hair is usually a frizzy mess when I wake up; now I have a glob of your disgusting gum stuck to the front of my bangs!"

When Dad decides that his gum is no longer worth chewing, he spits it into a tissue and neatly places it under the far corner of his pillow. Every now and then, a chunk of gum finds its way to my mother's side of the bed. "No matter how many times I scream at you about this disgusting habit, you insist that you must follow this pattern of pillow fluffing, crossword puzzle solving, gum chewing and wrapper throwing, or your patients would definitely suffer. Yeah, I bet they would," Mom blasted him.

If I destroyed his crossword puzzle, I'd feel really sorry for any patients he'd see the next day. I mean, a drill in the hand of a grumpy, edgy, sleepy dentist is a scary thought. If you add nasty, dopey, creepy, and doc, the seven dwarfs all rolled into one could be my father in the morning. So to protect Snow White and innocent patients, I copy my horoscope into my homework notebook instead. During lunch at school, I read it to my friends Erin, Marissa, and Amber.

Besides reading my daily horoscope, my other obsession is checking my mail for invitations. As soon as I open the door to my house at 11 Walnut Lane, I can't wait. It's the same every day: I step off the school bus, tell my best friend Marissa to call me, run to my house, open the door, and grab the mail. I'm pretty good at sizing up a day's delivery from ten feet away. I only live one block from the bus stop, so all of this happens pretty quickly. Marissa lives two blocks away, on Sycamore Lane, so it takes her a little longer to get home and check to see if any invitations are waiting for her.

Marissa and I made a pact, where we agreed to simultaneously open any official-looking envelopes, packages with glitter leaking out, colored oversized tubes, or fancy decorated boxes that are addressed to us. See, we're best friends, so that's the right thing to do.

Last year when I turned twelve, Mom bought me a large pink wicker basket with my name, **JODI**, painted in a magical shade of metallic silver on it. It sits beneath the side table in the front hall. If Mom sorts through the household mail before I get home, she drops my deliveries into this basket and they wait there patiently for my return from school.

Because I'm twelve years old, I am right smack at the beginning of the bar and bat mitzvah season. It's a Jewish tradition for boys to have a bar mitzvah after they turn thirteen. Girls can have a bat mitzvah when they turn twelve, but many wait till they're thirteen. It is a major religious ceremony. Nowadays, a lot of Jewish families celebrate afterward in a big way. We're not talking roller blading parties with a cookie cake from Mrs. Fields. We're talking out-of-the-box theme parties and over-the-top deejays and entertainers.

My birthday is November 18 and my bat mitzvah is set for January 22. According to my online psychic and long-range horoscope, this year will be like a roller coaster. The highs will be very high, but the lows might turn into total screw-ups. They warned me to be prepared for some startling discoveries and events during the next few months. I hope that means an A for once in math, little diamond stud earrings for my birthday present, and finding the secret recipe to becoming the most popular girl in the seventh grade. And, it wouldn't hurt if I could help solve the problem of homelessness, too.

As of this moment, I am so hoping for an invitation to Jason Kroc's bar mitzvah. Jason and I have been in the same class since first grade and he is now, without question, the hottest kid in seventh grade. He looks like he grew three inches over the summer when he was at soccer camp. My old friend hangs out with all the popular kids and is, like, on a mission to be voted the coolest ever. It's actually become his obsession.

He's like a totally different person from the Jason I used to know. He has the latest "look." You know, that long hair with bangs almost covering his eyes. He's constantly swishing them upward when he's talking to you. Would it be too aggressive of me to just flick his bangs back with my hand?

When I saw him at the lockers on the first day of school a couple of weeks ago, I couldn't believe my eyes. You should see how amazing his biceps look. "Stop staring," Amber said, as she poked me in the arm. But I couldn't help noticing that the bright blue shirt he was wearing matched his dreamy blue eyes. I think I went into some sort of trance.

"Whatever happened to skinny Jason Kroc who still sucked his thumb in third grade, and cried if his mother was more than two minutes late picking him up from school?" asked Amber. "And why does he flex his muscles when anyone looks in his direction? Come on!"

Anyway, I just started middle school last week and to put it mildly, it's no "piece-a-cake"! When I was in sixth grade at Cherry Valley Elementary School, I belonged to the coolest group of kids. My friends and I were the oldest kids in the school and we ran the show. Everyone looked up to us, and by the end of the year all of our teachers pretty much let us do our own thing. But now that I've graduated to Forrester Middle School, I am just a lowly seventh grader who gets no respect from the older kids. Kids can be kind of scary at F.M.S. I've seen a bunch of eighth graders picking on kids my age and it wasn't pretty. They told the seventh grade green team to wear purple on the third color day, if they wanted to be extra-cool and hang out with the eighth graders after school.

"You fools look like the 'Fruit of the Loom' grapes," Michael Canister said to the group, whose faces had all turned the color green. The joke was certainly on them.

I guess I'm lucky, because most of the time the kids don't hassle me. I do get called "shrimp" from time to time, but I guess it comes with the territory. After all, I'm only four feet eleven inches tall. "Don't worry so much about your height now, Jodi," Mom told me. "You should have a growth spurt any day now. After all, I am five feet and a half, and look how much we have in common." She could be right. So far, I have her very curly dirty blonde hair and her not-so-delightful frizz. Without the help of our favorite hair gels and mousse which we comb through our knots, we would be lost.

Let's not forget about Dad's DNA. I inherited his hazel eyes. Depending on the color of my outfit, they change colors. In some ways I'm like a chameleon. I like to think of my eyes as being two cool mood rings. You know, the ones that mutate depending on whether I am sad or happy, or whatever my mood happens to be. And my mood changes a lot, depending on my astrological forecast.

If the planet Jupiter is rising in my sign, I'm likely to be in a blue funk all day. Don't even think about looking at me, talking to me, or—heaven forbid—asking a favor. Once, I found my eight-year-old brother, Seth, scrounging through my desk drawer to borrow a ruler and I totally freaked. I lost it so badly that I dragged him into the basement and threatened to lock him in my moldy old camp trunk. However, when Mars is sinking into Scorpio, you'll not find a nicer, more considerate Jodi. I remember the time that I gave up a Saturday night out with my friends to play video games with snotty-nosed little

Seth. See how changeable I can be? That was the same night my friends got to see Hannah Montana at the Forrester Center for the Performing Arts.

Can you believe that I turned down a backstage pass to clean up green boogers? It's just amazing what effect the stars have on me.

Because I know so much about astrology, I feel it is my job to help my best friends with their daily horoscopes. I put myself in charge of interpreting their daily horoscopes during lunch every day. Sometimes, I even leave notes in their lockers to warn them if major disasters are coming. We also have nightly instant messaging sessions to totally take care of last-minute emergencies. It lets Amber, Marissa, Erin, and me feel like we have more control over any school crises—or, if not control, we at least have a handle on what to look out for on any given day, how to react, and what we should look forward to.

I'm feeling very lucky today because my horoscope said my dreams would be fulfilled. I am hoping it means that I'll be chosen for the girls' soccer team. The tryouts are after school, and I can already see myself wearing our school colors, purple and white. I'm not the most athletic, but I'm going to give it my all. I'm not going to even think about the last time I crashed into Marissa, at camp, when we were both going after the same ball. It wasn't a pretty sight. But you never know; I might make the team anyway. It'll be great. Marissa thinks I want to make the team only so I can be near Jason. She's crazy. Wish me luck!

* * *

CHAPTER 2
COLORS

Today's Horoscope:

Scorpio (October 24–November 22) Excellent time to spend with friends. A neglected relationship reveals new possibilities. The cosmic clock is ticking and it is important to create a good impression. Today is a red-letter day.

"Time to rise and shine, and greet this beautiful, crisp morning! The leaves will be changing soon, so zip up those new sweaters or grab a jacket before you jump on the school bus!" shouted Max of *Max in the Morning* from the clock radio.

No problem, Max. The last thing I need today is to have a fashion malfunction. Oh, wait. I forgot today is color day. Last night, my online fashion horoscope advised me of what I should wear today, and RED is the color. I'd better call Marissa.

"Marissa, I have a problem. I know that today is color day at school and I am supposed to wear orange for my team, but my horoscope is screaming for me to wear red. I set out my new red corduroy jacket, a white tank top, my black low-riding jeans, and my favorite red suede ankle boots last night. What should I do?"

"Get a grip, Jodi. Where is it written that you can't mix red and orange?" said Marissa over the phone. "I have to finish getting dressed or I'll miss the bus. You'll figure it out. But I have to quickly tell you that my mother bought me a new red leather hobo bag. Wait until you see it!"

My new middle school organizes each grade into teams, and each team is represented by a color. A team consists of about twenty-five students each. Because there are a hundred or so kids in each grade, four colors were chosen: blue, orange, green, and red. I'm on the orange team and Jason is on blue. Lately, he has started wearing every shade in denim: faded, dark, bleached, etc. I'm not just talking about his jeans. It's right down to his socks, sneakers, laces, and braces.

He has even taken this color theme to a new level by handing in his assignments on blue paper. It's beginning to be embarrassing, but he is super-proud of himself. His new friends have started to copy him, which only makes Jason look that much more popular. They've even gone so far as to put blue streaks in their hair, and some have painted a stripe of navy blue nail polish down the center of their pinkies. When they showed up at school waving their fingers in everyone's face, they were warned that they'd be suspended if they didn't use some serious nail polish remover. How lame! It was silly enough on Ozzie Osborne, why would anybody want to copy that? Even more ridiculous, a group went to the preseason football game with half their faces painted in a ghastly shade of what looked like a blueberry Slushie. They may look like idiots, but at least they have school spirit.

The big rage you spot in the school halls these days are gold or silver chain-link necklaces. All the cool guys wear them. Jason has one, but leave it to him to find a silver-blue metallic necklace. It really stands out.

I haven't been invited over to Jason's house in so long, I'm sure it looks totally different now. I can just picture what his bedroom must look like today. The cute weirdo probably has designer denim wallpaper, wall-to-wall ropy-looking carpeting, a blue-and-white striped comforter, and a pale blue laptop computer on his desk. Let's not forget the blue basketball hoop hung over his door, the blue i-pod hung on his belt clip, and his aqua see-through jam jacket hard shell case for his i-phone , that is always in his hand. Mrs. Kroc most likely serves his afternoon snack of blue Gatorade and blue frosted cupcakes on a blue flowered china plate. Ooh…it sounds so '70s. I am ready to puke from all this blue. Maybe it's a good thing that I haven't been invited.

I always try my best to wear at least something orange to school on color day. I have orange striped knee-highs and a cute coral threaded bracelet that are my standbys. I'm on the hunt for an orange headband, hoop earrings, or a patent leather hobo bag to complete my color day outfit.

My friends and I went to the local flea market one Sunday, where we found a table that had all sorts of adorable jewelry. That orange bangle bracelet was calling my name and it only cost $4.50. Marissa bought a ruby-red toe ring made from stretchy fish string that matches her auburn hair. Lucky for her, she's on the red team. Erin bought an emerald green rhinestone ear clip to wear at the green team's pep rallies. The fourth member of my BFF's (Best Friends Forever), Amber, bought a dozen bangles in every color you can imagine because she feels this team color nonsense separates people. Amber is above these school competitions, doesn't care that she is on the green team, and wishes everyone would just get along.

At the last Forrester Falcons home soccer game against our rival, the Glenview Gulls, the bleachers looked like someone had painted wide colored stripes across the seats. Each section had rows and rows of cheering students dressed in blue, orange, red, or green, all frantically waving their colored pom-poms or banners.

"Look at Amber, guys," said Erin. "She has been changing her seat after every quarter. Instead of pom-poms or a banner, she's waving a gigantic peacock feather fan over her head. She is such a character."

The multicolored fan broke up the color scheme, and everyone around her started to boo and yell at Amber. This was the exact response she had hoped for, and it only made her laugh. She then would pick herself up and move to the next section, to annoy her next group of victims. Erin, Marissa, and I just adore Amber for her independent nature. Her protests crack us up.

The rivalry in the seventh grade has gone well beyond colors. The latest battle for the best team was a writing competition on the topic, "In 300 words or less, explain why students feel the need to get body piercing and tattoos." Duh! I would be so afraid to walk into one those filthy tattoo parlors. Besides, my mother would kill me, and then there's good old "Dentist Do-Right" Dad.

Picture this: One night at the dinner table, I open my mouth to ask Dad to pass the cheesy bread sticks and my shiny new sterling silver tongue stud momentarily blinds him. Think how crazy he would get. In fact, one of his dental assistants was dumb enough to show up for work after having a gold ring put through her lower lip. Dad fired her on the spot.

Just last night, I saw a TV news program that showed—in way too much detail—the horrible complications that mouth, tongue, and lip piercing can cause. You can chip your teeth, get an infection in your tongue or mouth, and even lose your taste buds. Why would anyone risk that?

At the local supermarket, there's a girl that works at the checkout counter who has over twenty piercings in and around her tongue and lips. When she tells you how much you owe, it always sounds the same, "Smirthy-free flothy-fleur" or "frouny-suuth" or "aigthy-nie." Don't ask me what she means; I just hand her a ten-dollar bill and hope for the right amount of change.

I have been craving one of those cute little belly-button rings forever. "Not while I'm your mother," Mom said, when she saw the mouth-pierced and tattooed sales clerk. With my mother's old-fashioned thinking and my father's rigid attitude, that's probably not in the cards for me. I'll have to work on that.

School pep rallies, soccer matches, cheerleading try-outs, science fairs, spelling bees, and even rounds of *Jeopardy* games—they're taking over my life! Personally, I think the color war at school has gotten way out hand. The plus side of the competitions is that I get the opportunity to see Jason when the orange team defends itself against the blue team.

Except lately, it seems that is the only time Jason and I ever run into each other. Guess his new circle of friends no longer includes me. He doesn't seem to have time for me like he used to. I feel like I'm out of the loop. I hope that he's simply very busy, and not avoiding me on purpose. But even so, I'd better be invited to his bar mitzvah, which is just around the corner. Oh, make it today, please! I must be invited!

With my luck, the only invitation that will be sitting in my basket today will be for Tiffany Cooper's birthday bash. I have to tell you about Tiffany Cooper, one of the most annoying creatures on the planet. Tiffany is unfortunately on the orange team. Instead of keeping true to the rest of us by wearing anything remotely connected to the color orange, she has to dress in pink chic. Tiffany feels she is far above our cheesy school tradition. If she would act like Amber, who demonstrates her independent streak in amusing ways, it would be bearable. She sticks up her nose at middle school events because she thinks she's better than everyone else. Instead of having my best friends or Jason in most of my classes, I got stuck with Tiffany in almost all of them. How unfair.

Tiffany's birthday party is always the first major happening of the school year. It's become an annual event. I think she wishes her birthday would become a national holiday. She's an only child, and her parents seem to think that she deserves a birthday party extravaganza every year. I remember when she turned five. The Coopers hosted such a huge party; they hired all these Disney characters and rock-singer look-alikes. It was awesome. I remember thinking that I was actually at Disney World, and cried when my mom said it was time to go home.

I can't believe I was so dumb back then. For my fifth birthday, Mom and Dad took me, Becky, and three of my friends to McDonald's for lunch. Mom brought a star-shaped cake that had sparklers instead of candles. I wished for a Daredevil Barbie Doll and actually got her, along with a brand-new shiny red bicycle. Believe it or not, it's still one of my favorite birthday memories.

The gossip this year is that Tiffany's parents felt bad that they couldn't throw a bat mitzvah party for her like her Jewish friends will be having. The Coopers are Christian, not Jewish. Anyway I heard from a very reliable source that they are planning the ultimate "faux mitzvah" party for their daughter's thirteenth birthday. They are trying to set a record for all the parties that follow this year. It's just so wannabee. Becoming a bar or bat mitzvah is not supposed to be about the party. It's a religious ceremony that symbolizes a boy's or girl's passage into adulthood. I don't understand why Tiffany's parents always have to turn things into a competition and make a big to-do. I wouldn't want anyone to make fun of a meaningful occasion like a bat mitzvah. Oh-oh. This sounds like one of the rabbi's sermons. Stop me now!

I'll just slip on this coral bracelet, and off I go to catch the bus.

* * *

CHAPTER 3
PREDICTIONS

 Today's Horoscope:

Scorpio (October 24–November 22) Buckle up! Extreme planetary action will soon create sudden twists and bumps in life's highways. This week there won't be a dull or predictable moment for Scorpio.

After an uneventful September school day, I came home and grabbed the mail from my mail basket. I tore through the few letters from Aunt Tillie, this month's *Teen Spirit* magazine, and a *Star Signs* catalogue. There it was: the invitation to Jason Kroc's bar mitzvah! I tore open the camouflage print envelope. The khaki stationery announced October 19, 2007, as the date for the big event.

"Great! This is what I've been waiting for, for forever!" I screamed.

"What are you waving above your head?" laughed Mom. "And what a mess you are making. It looks like tiny paper alligator confetti is falling out. Jodi, stop shaking that envelope. The little lizards are getting stuck in your hair, and they are all over the floor, too."

"I don't mind making a mess because I'm so happy. I'll clean up all the baby crocs, but first I have to call Marissa and see if she got her invitation to Jason's bar mitzvah, too."

I immediately speed-dialed Marissa Torlucci's phone number. We had planned to get together as soon as the invitations came, to check the astrological forecast for the bar mitzvah's date. Marissa got to my house so quickly you'd have thought she'd been transported by some sort of laser beam.

My room could not have provided a better mood for the project we were about to undertake. I had spent endless hours making sure it was decorated to give me the feeling of living in the zodiac, with Scorpio as the featured attraction. My fluffy sand-colored comforter is the shade of my favorite arthropod, while the walls are painted a soft beige, giving the room an earthy, desert-like atmosphere. The ceiling is black, and it is covered with silver and gold drawings of Scorpio, the scorpion, Leo the lion, Pisces the fish, Taurus the bull, Cancer the crab, and the other seven astrological sun signs.

"Even though I've been in your room a thousand times, it amazes me. Other zodiac lovers would die to live here," said Marissa.

I thanked her for the compliment, but I still feel like the room is missing something. I can't wrap my head around what would make the room feel more perfect.

"Marissa, turn on my new Fray CD." My grandparents bought me a new sound system for my twelfth birthday. It has six different types of sounds and all these different settings that can change the mood, for studying, sleeping, or just daydreaming. I can listen to soothing ocean waves hitting the shore, birds in a tropical rain forest, or plain "white noise" that blocks out the annoying voices of my sister and brother.

"Open up the closet door, Marissa, I have to show you how I reorganized my closet last weekend."

"Dude, this really rocks," said Marissa in awe. "One shelf is lined with multicolored candles, incense sticks and holders, and an assorted selection of tea leaves. On another shelf you have sets of tarot cards, stones carved with ancient rune symbols, your Ouija board, and…is that a new crystal ball?"

"Since you were here the last time, I bought more fortune-telling goodies. Check out the new books on astrology, mysticism, star charting, numerology, and palm reading on the third and fourth shelves."

"Can I pick the candles that we need to use for our astrological investigation?" Marissa asked. "Here are three citrus-ginger scented candles, to represent you, me, and Jason. This aroma therapy combination is just the right thing with its invigorating and energizing powers. Jodi, I am adding some mandarin orange incense sticks for good measure. We have some serious work ahead of us"

"What is the obnoxious stench coming from this room?" shrieked Becky, as she burst into my room.

"What gives? Ever heard of knocking?"

"I just came in to tell you how great I did on the soccer field today. I scored three goals and had five assists and was MVP. I'm, like, totally wiped. Don't disturb me; I'm going to my room to chill out. And this smell of orange reeks! It is making me feel like I'm going to lose my lunch!" yelled Becky.

"Your sister Becky thinks she is a prom queen. She's always tossing that perfect hair of hers," said Marissa, after Becky left the room.

She's more of a drama queen.

Becky, Becky, Becky, Becky. She's a Capricorn because her birthday is January 10. According to her chart, she is a goat. And I don't mean that nicely. Her sign indicates that she is cool, stubborn, bossy, a good problem solver, and a natural athlete. Because of Capricorn's great organizational skills, she is able to work on several projects at the same time and still make the Honor Roll. Goats also tend to have mood swings, and believe me, I could write a whole novel on how nasty she can be to me when she gets into one of her moods.

You know, having a big sister like Becky isn't easy. She is about five feet six inches tall. And I have to admit she's pretty and has it together. Her light brown hair falls in the perfect flip, which she usually flings around to draw attention to herself. I think it's a way to get the boys to look at her. It just drives me nuts the way she's always tossing her head like that. You'd think she was trying out for a L'Oreal commercial. I could never get my kinky hair to do that. And to make matters worse, she's always bragging that she needed a bra before her twelfth birthday! I'll be lucky if I need a bra by the time I'm fifteen.

Did I mention how competitive Becky is in school? Well, she is, and she's not just out for blood with grades. She's also a star player on the girls' high school soccer and volleyball teams. I, on the other hand, have no interest in playing aggressive sports and am happy to support my school teams by going to the games and pep rallies. Did I forget to tell you that I did NOT make the middle school soccer team? I guess my horoscope was a bit off that day. At least I tried. I'll give myself an A for effort.

Unlike Becky, I'm a Scorpio because my birthday is November 18. And hey, we couldn't be more opposite. These signs are as different as night and day. According to my chart, Scorpios are caring, introspective, and seemingly self-controlled. However, don't let that fool you. They can be aggressive and intense as well.

I think I'll light another candle just for spite.

Who does she think she is? Just because Becky's my older sister doesn't make her my boss.

"I can't believe Becky has the nerve to just barge into my room. We need our privacy, Marissa. I may not be an athlete or an overachiever like perfect Becky. It's not who I am. But I am great when it comes to astrology. Becky may be a Capricorn, but I am proud to be a Scorpio."

"Jodi, I'm so psyched. Let's get to work. We have to research what the stars have in store for us on October nineteenth, Jason's bar mitzvah date. You know that what we discover will determine what outfits we should wear, where we will be sitting, and even how we should behave that night," explained Marissa.

"Let's start with my deck of tarot cards. Since the tarot deck is used mainly as a tool to forecast the future, this is exactly what we need to begin with. Our mission is simple: I need to know if Jason and I are meant to be together." Marissa shuffled the deck and laid out the top three cards face down from left to right. "These three cards will represent my past, present, and future. Turn over the future card first."

"Oh, no way! This is so rad; I picked the number six card which means 'the lovers.'"

"Shut up! Yes, I knew Jason and I are meant to be together."

"Don't jump to conclusions, Jodi. How do we know that the lovers are you and Jason?" asked Marissa. "Do you really think this card means that you two will be a couple? All we know is that you will come in contact with at least one well-matched couple in your future. Maybe I am one half of that perfect couple. I've had my eye on Peter Spatler since last week when he scored two goals at the soccer match. Let's finish the reading to figure out the whole picture," my friend added.

"Marissa, sometimes you are a bit too negative. Can't you let me have some fun? I'm going to light two more candles."

"Not negative, Jodes, realistic. I'm still not sure what you see in the guy anyway. As far as I can tell, Jason doesn't seem to care about you or his other friends anymore. But look, it's getting late. It's time to channel Scarlet Skye, our favorite online fortune-teller."

We took off our shoes and jumped on my bed. The fluffy comforter made the perfect setting for us to open the *Ephemeris*, a book used by astrologers to calculate the positions of the signs and the planets to forecast events into the next century. This book is usually used by adults before they sign contracts, buy houses or cars, purchase expensive items like jewelry, or even when they start a new business. Scarlet Skye, the well-known astrologer who has her own website, had suggested that this was the book for our predictions.

* * *

Over the summer, when we surfed the web and found Scarlet's site, the passage that had special meaning for the two of us was: "If you are a daily reader of the horoscope section of your local newspaper, you are only getting a small part of the picture. Sun signs like Leo, Pisces, and Capricorn are too general. These horoscopes pertain to anyone who is born in that month. Moon placement is more important, and you want to find out about the atmosphere."

Another book, which I found on Amazon, is *The Astrological Guidebook for the 21st Century*, written by Dr. Howard Crowley. He is famous for his predictions about well-known politicians, sports figures, and rock stars. He wrote this handbook for predicting people's lives according to their birth chart. This is why it is so important to know the exact time a person was born. "Forewarned is forearmed" is his motto. I loved it so much that I begged my mom to hire someone to hand-paint it on the wall above my bed. The artist painted it in script with gold metallic paint.

* * *

"I don't have to convince you, Jodi, that all this astrology stuff is not hocus-pocus. It's serious," said Marissa, as she continued to scan through Scarlet Skye's website.

Once, when one of her clients needed help with a man she was dating, Scarlet did a mini-analysis on his personality. The astrologer picked up negative and suspicious character traits. He had an unlisted telephone number, refused to meet for even coffee at a local Starbucks, and said he didn't have a recent photo of himself. Red flag! He was history. The client ended up marrying a man who was much more compatible with her, on February 14, Valentine's Day. This date was picked because the moon and the sun were in the fixed signs of Virgo and

Aquarius, suggesting a steady position that blended with the newlyweds' birth charts.

Over the next two hours, we investigated our charts and figured out that the night of Jason's bar mitzvah was going to be on the wild side, with surprises galore. I found myself transported into a magical ballroom, slow dancing, with Jason's arms wrapped around me.

"I'm having trouble concentrating, Jodi. I'm worried about completing our science project on the family tree. For some reason, my parents are not being very helpful. I've asked them simple questions. I don't know why they can't just give me simple answers. Seems like they keep inventing weird excuses to avoid answering me. I was hoping that this assignment was going to be easy because I want to get an A in Science," said Marissa, as she began to stuff things into her backpack.

Just then, the phone rang. "Hey, Jodes, did you get Jason's invite?" asked Heath.

"Who's on the phone?" questioned Marissa.

Covering the mouthpiece, I said nobody important.

"I'm very busy right now, Heath. I'll talk to you at school tomorrow morning."

"Was that Heath Berman who called? I saw him at soccer practice last week," said Marissa. "He's not as bad-looking or as geeky as he was in elementary school. If he would let his thick, dark brown hair grow a little longer and lose the dorky glasses, he would give Jason something to worry about."

"Would you stop? Jason is the only one for me."

* * *

CHAPTER 4
FAMILY TREE

 Today's Horoscope:

Scorpio (October 24–November 22) Wake up, little sleepy-head. With so many issues to tackle it may be tough to decide where to begin. Give school projects your best effort and focus on family matters in the days to come.

"Jodi, come down for breakfast, please! You don't want to be late for school!" Mom hollered from downstairs.

Mom's really great. She still gets my breakfast ready every morning.

Amazing! She has a master's degree in education from UCLA and was teaching third grade, but met my dad the summer after her first year of teaching. Before she knew it, she was married and moving to New Jersey.

Even though my mom doesn't teach full time anymore, she's been doing some tutoring at home and has substituted at the local elementary school for the last two years. She keeps threatening to go back to work full time, but hasn't. I'm not sure she really wants to.

Anyway, my mom is pretty cool for being forty-five years old. She was born and raised in Los Angeles. She used to roller skate along the boardwalk on Venice Beach. They didn't have roller blades when she was growing up. I wish I could snap my fingers and go back in time, so that we could skate along the beach together and maybe run into some movie stars who were just hanging out. It must be so cool to grow up in a city full of famous people.

"Jodi! Did you hear me? Your eggs are getting cold!" Mom screamed impatiently.

"Just a minute, Mom. I'll be right down. I'm just fixing my hair. It's out of control this morning and frizzing big-time. Give me a minute, please!"

My mom of all people should understand about the trauma of having such frizzy hair. She never leaves the house without spending an hour blow-drying her hair. It's naturally curly, like mine, but she won't just let it go natural. She's funny like that. She puts enough mousse and straightening gels in it that some days I think her hair might just break in half!

It's amazing how much time she can spend in her bathroom. But no one beats my sister Becky. Our bathroom might as well be her living room, with all the time she stays in there. She does have the latest teen magazines and books on beauty tips. I love to read the pages that she tabs with purple Post-it notes, to get the inside scoop on what Becky thinks are the "gotta-have-its." She's always right on.

Once, Mom paid $500 and spent five hours getting this Japanese hair-straightening treatment so her hair would look as silky as Becky's. She went into New York City for this, of course. It stayed pretty straight for five weeks and then *sproing*! The kink was back. Dad said she should have insisted on getting her money back, but she never even tried. I wouldn't mind getting extensions in my hair, like Britney Spears. But, I read in *Teen Scene* that they cost $2,800 and take nine hours of sitting still in a beauty parlor chair. Yeah, like that would ever happen.

Another thing that troubles my mother lately is her weight. She is five feet five and a half and was considered a skinny kid growing up. Now, she says she's approaching "the change" and slowly expanding at the waist. Expanding? I think of balloons or air pumps, not people when I hear that word. I'm still trying to figure out what that means exactly. She says that she just can't get away with eating the way she used to. She says that even looking at donuts makes her gain weight!

The most outrageous thing she ever did during one of her diets was to tape a donut to her thigh. She said this reminded her that the calories would simply end up as fat on her thighs. Looking at and feeling the donut taped to her leg reminded her NOT to eat anything fattening. Do you know that one day, at Becky's soccer practice, I saw her sneak three chocolate Bavarian cream-filled donuts, even though the original donut was still taped to her leg? I caught her eating the third one, and she made some excuse about having just "a bite." That is so second grade!

Anyway, don't get me wrong, Mom's not fat at all, just a little overweight. I don't dare ask her how much she weighs. I figure she'd be too sensitive to answer me. She recently started buying pants with stretch waists instead of the ones with zippers. I asked her about this, and she went rambling on about "water weight."

So, I looked up "water weight" at www.webstersdictionary. com. I couldn't find the definition of it, but found the word "water-logged." It means to fill or soak with water, as to be heavy or hard to manage. That figures. It didn't say anything about women and elasticized waist pants. Nothing! I'm convinced that when women turn forty they must discover this new secret language for moms, which makes it impossible for their kids and husbands to have any idea what they're saying 95 percent of the time. I know this will happen to me when I turn forty. It's really freaking me out.

"Jodi, I'm not kidding this time. Get down here now, or I'm throwing out your breakfast!" Mom shouted.

Entering the kitchen, I saw Seth finishing his bowl of Cheerios. Many were scattered on the floor, and milk splotches covered the front of his shirt. So typical of him. Usually, by this time most of his apple juice would have soaked through the placemat and would have been dripping down the side of the kitchen table, and he did not disappoint his fans this morning. I keep telling my mom to buy industrial-strength paper towels to cover the table and the floor when he sits down to eat.

"Seth, give your mother a break! Do you think that it's possible for you to swallow more than you spill? On second thought, it's probably better that you don't get to drink all of that sickeningly sweet juice. It's just going to destroy your teeth or make you throw up," said Dad, as he grabbed the morning paper.

* * *

My brother, Seth, has been a little monster from the start. The moment Mom set eyes on him, his red baby face was scrunched up tight, and he started screaming like he wanted to get out of the hospital nursery as fast as possible, to cause some trouble. And believe me, the nurses were happy to see him go. In the hospital, the pediatrician announced, "Congratulations, Sharon! You've got a real live one here! Get ready. He's going to be a handful." Mom was furious. What kind of insensitive doctor had she selected for my new brother?

The pediatrician was right on. Seth had colic. That's something like a 24/7 upset stomach, along with gas pains and nausea. Babies with colic always cry. I don't mean little whimpers. They sound like they might be dying. And sometimes it doesn't seem to ever stop. Mom said his colic made him have lots of throw-ups, and we're not talking little spit-ups here!

I remember when my family once went to a fancy, grown-up restaurant to celebrate Becky's ninth birthday. The White Bistro had white linen tablecloths and fresh white orchids placed everywhere. Mom and Dad ordered their favorite, very expensive red wine to go with their lamb chops. Becky was acting all mature, wearing her new green velvet dress. At the end of the meal, we were just about to be served our white chocolate mousse dessert when suddenly, a tidal wave of green puke spurted out across the table from Seth's mouth, like a volcanic eruption. His cute little baby mouth was suddenly transformed into a large geyser, the likes of which no human had ever seen, or even imagined!

Well, I don't want to make you sick by describing what our table looked like, but the vomit was all over poor Becky's pretty dress. Some flecks even found their way into her hair. I never saw us leave a restaurant as fast as we did that night. I don't even know how Mom did it, but before you could say "'boo" we were in the car and heading home. No one was speaking, and guess what? Little Sethy-poo was sound asleep, looking all angelic and everything. Peaceful as a lamb. I don't think Mom took him to a restaurant for another three years. My family jokes around and says that the owners of the White Bistro should have changed the name to the Greenhouse.

I don't want to forget Seth's temper tantrums, screaming, and excessive clinging. You get the picture. It set the tone for the months to come. After having Becky and me, the model children, how could Seth be so difficult? It's funny how many showers Mom took, so she wouldn't hear his screeching. Dad frequently brought home new moisturizers, because Mom's once-smooth skin was beginning to look more like that of a scaly iguana.

"I'm not really hungry this morning, Mom. I'll eat a lot at lunch instead. I'll just grab a couple bites of these eggs and take the English muffin with me on the bus."

The Forrester Middle School bus was coming into sight, but I managed to run the last two blocks in record time. As I took my usual seat next to Marissa on the bus, she said, "How's it going? I'm so excited about all the parties coming up. Tiffany's bogus party is just around the corner and I don't even have a dress picked out yet. Of course, I want to look great for the first party of the year."

"More than that, Marissa, I really want to knock Jason out when I make my entrance at his bar mitzvah."

"Jodes, I have something else on my mind that I need to talk to you about. Can we drop the discussion about Jason and what we're going to wear to his party for a second? What really has me freaked out today is our science project. Ms. Beeker's assignment to create a family tree is causing me some serious stress," said Marissa. "We have to research our family's names, dates of births and deaths, husbands or wives, children, and even where they were born, going back as many generations as possible.

"I keep asking my parents for some info about our ancestors, and for some reason they have been making all these lame excuses about being too busy to help me. I'm getting some really strange vibes here," continued Marissa.

"Don't be ridiculous. There's probably nothing to worry about, but let's check out your Month-at-a-Glance Horoscope on the web later. I'm glad you reminded me about this assignment, because I have questions of my own to ask my folks, too. I've been trying to figure out why Dad is so tall, because his father and grandfather were only a little taller than Becky. Ms. Beeker said we'd be learning all about genes this week. I have no clue what a recessive or dominant gene is. Do you?"

* * *

CHAPTER 5
GENES AND JEANS

 Today's Horoscope:

Scorpio (October 24–November 22) You are operating under weird astro-flows, the sort that bring strange events, intense dreams, and unusual reactions. Leap into action and get things done early in the day.

"What in the world are you doing, Brent?" shrieked Ms. Beeker. "Stop drinking from the eyewash spigot. It is not a water fountain, young man!"

Brent Walters took one last gulp, and with water dribbling down his shirt, he said to Jason, "You owe me five bucks. I told you I would take your dare." He smirked as he swaggered back to his seat in the science lab.

"Can you believe how moronic Jason's new friends are?" asked Amber. "Take a look at Brent's head. He's shaved a zigzag through the back of his hair. What an idiot!"

I can't concentrate on this now. How do my looks compare to my parents? Why am I so short? Why am I so uncoordinated? How did Becky get such silky-smooth hair?

"Jodi, are you with us? You look like you're daydreaming again," said Erin, giving me a gentle shove.

Ms. Beeker was at the blackboard, lecturing on and on about how genes determine what color hair or eyes a person has. "They also affect his or her height, weight, and even the length of one's nose," she continued.

* * *

Being four foot eleven isn't as bad as it might seem. In fact, my mom still says that I'll definitely get taller. When she turned thirteen, she had a growth spurt. She grew three inches in six months to reach five feet five and a half inches, her present height. Maybe I'll grow four more inches, but then I still wouldn't be as tall as Becky. But anything's possible.

My eyes aren't bad, though. My mom is always complimenting me on them. She says they are one of my best features. When I have a tan in the summer, they are swimming-pool green, but the rest of the year they turn a darker shade of forest green. Another good characteristic that I inherited from my parents is my father's fitness gene. Dad is really into exercise, even though he is naturally thin, like I am. Sometimes when we are out for a walk, he'll drop to the ground for no reason and do twenty push-ups and then fifty sit-ups. It's a bit bizarre, but it works for him.

At six foot one, he weighs only 185 pounds. He must get on the scale every morning to make sure that he hasn't gained an ounce. If he weighs one pound over, he announces that he's going to jog after work. Then he adds "No dessert for me tonight, Sharon." My mother answers him by rolling her eyes in his direction. So weird.

* * *

"I hope you all are paying attention to this material. I think this class is due for one of my famous pop quizzes," Ms. Beeker said threateningly.

I leaned toward Amber and whispered, "This is so incredibly stressful. The last thing I feel like spending my time doing is studying for another stupid test. I have so much on my mind and so little time. On top of my schoolwork, I also have to start studying for my bat mitzvah, and I haven't even begun thinking about what I'm going to do for my community service requirement. My rabbi calls it a tzedakah project."

"Girls, please stop the chatter, or would you like the quiz right now?" asked Ms. Beeker. "This is not Cherry Valley Elementary School, young ladies. We do not tolerate talking during class in middle school!"

* * *

Being a seventh grader is a real challenge, like I said before. Fortunately, my three best friends are making this first year at F.M.S. more bearable. We go way back.

Marissa is my very best friend. We met in preschool. Hard to believe it's been that long. We've had our ups and downs, but mostly we've been pretty tight. Our biggest fallout was in third grade. Odd, how I can still remember the fight. We all had to make shadow boxes of some type, to do with an outer-space scene. I thought it'd be a cinch, since my mom used to teach science and I'd get lots of help. Then Marissa showed up with her project. It was the coolest one I had ever seen. It looked like a professional artist had designed it. The planets in her solar system actually rotated! She had a fan set up that produced a constant wind flow. There were small spheres for the planets and everything was scaled to size. She had a miniature space shuttle orbiting the earth and an authentic replica of the space station. It was pure genius!

She got the only A+ in the class, and made such a big deal about it that I accused her of cheating—and I said it in front of the teacher! I'll never forget how bad I felt after those words came out of my mouth. To this day, I'm not even sure why I did it; I guess I was just really jealous. I mean, my mom was a science teacher. My project should have been the best. Mine was very boring, more like total dullsville compared to hers. We didn't speak for a week. I can remember how miserable I felt.

Fortunately, I believe that our friendship is destined by the stars and not really something we have much control over. We made up. Marissa forgave me after I wrote her a two-page apology letter. I don't think we've had an argument since. She says she wants to be an astronaut when she grows up. I have no idea what I want to be. Lately, I don't seem to have a good grip on who I am. You see, I'm not into outer space, but as I said earlier, I am really into astrology and all the supernatural stuff. Numerology fascinates me. Tarot cards are so intriguing. I love my collection of crystals and my great-smelling candles. I've been following my star chart since third grade. My friends all call me "The Star Gazer." I never make any major decisions without first consulting my chart. Never. Being friends with Marissa was simply destined to happen.

Let me tell you about her. Her parents are first-generation Americans, but according to Marissa, her grandparents on both sides were born in Italy. One side was from northern Italy and the other from the south, near Naples. That's how she explains why she has dark hair and olive skin, even though her parents are both very fair-skinned. She's taller than I am, but then again, most of my friends are. She must be almost five foot two already and is still growing. It's infuriating sometimes; she looks so grown-up and I still look like a little girl.

I keep asking my mom when I'm going to start looking more grown-up, but she just shrugs her shoulders and says, "Being short is good for a woman. You'll never have to worry about being too tall for your husband. You'll always be able to wear the most beautiful high heels. Just wait. You'll see. You're actually luckier being short."

I might be smaller, but I'm a little older than Marissa. Her birthday is December 20. She is so lucky that she was born before January 1! You see, in my school district the cutoff for starting kindergarten is the first of January. If she'd been born eleven days later, Marissa would have been in a different grade and well, perhaps we never would have met. It was fate. It was in the stars that we were meant to be in the same preschool class and be best friends. Sometimes, I think we were sisters in a former life. Not sisters like Becky and me, but really close. The kind that get along all the time and share clothes, as well as their deepest, darkest secrets.

Erin Guzman is my second closest friend. She's Jewish, like me. Her family goes to the same synagogue as mine does, and we've always been in Sunday school together. She has short black hair and green eyes, like a cat! She is tiny, like I am, so we can borrow each other's clothes. Like I said, my sister Becky never lets me do that. She won't even let me in her room anymore without asking permission. You'd think she had boys hiding in there! Erin is one of the sweetest girls I've ever met. She is always doing the nicest things for people. I remember on my tenth birthday, she made me a friendship bracelet and wrote a poem to go along with it.

> *A hug is the perfect gift for a friend like you.*
> *A hug comes in all sizes, colors and shapes,*
> *Whenever I'm sad or lonely,*
> *I think of how great a friend you are to me.*
> *Here's a hug for your birthday.*
> *Don't try to exchange it.*

Then there's Amber. Amber Ferris. Her dad is an ex-football player and her mom is the high school P.E. teacher. Amber is tall, too. Her mother refers to her as "big-boned." Amber says it's as if she's describing a dinosaur, and she doesn't want to be compared to a massive, extinct animal. She does use her size to make sure her opinions are heard loud and clear. Amber is also a fabulous basketball player, which is not surprising. She's already five foot four and only twelve years old!

* * *

"Get away from that refrigerator, Brent. If you don't return to your seat immediately, you're looking at a two-week suspension," said an exasperated Ms. Beeker.

But it was too late. Brent had already opened the lab refrigerator door and grabbed a jar containing the remains of a frog that had been dissected yesterday by the ninth grade class. The frog's body parts were floating in a vile-smelling, green formaldehyde solution. And Brent was staring at the gaping back of Amber's low-riding jeans. They would make the perfect receptacle for his latest prank.

Another one of Jason's friends, Sean Taylor, picked up on what Brent was planning to do. He decided to create a disturbance at the exact time that the amphibian was scheduled to be dropped down Amber's pants. He snatched a small vial of mercury that Jason had been playing with all period long. Jason had been fooling around with paper clips during the class lecture. He had unfolded two of them and had carefully inserted them through the cork stopper of the tube that contained the mercury.

Racing to the closest electrical outlet, Sean jammed the metal paperclips that were sticking out of the mercury into the socket. A sudden flash of light preceded an explosion that plunged the lab into momentary darkness.

The lights turned back on about fifteen seconds later, but by this time the entire class was screaming.

"Calm down, everybody! Don't anyone move," ordered Ms. Beeker. "Is everyone okay?" she asked.

The students all looked around at one another to see what had caused the commotion. Jason, Brent, and Sean were sitting still, like three little angels, but Amber had jumped out of her seat and was hysterical.

"I think there is something down my pants!" she yelled. "Get it out, now!"

I dashed to my friend's side, and then asked Ms. Beeker if I could take Amber to the girls' restroom.

"Go ahead, this class is turning into a three-ring circus anyway," said our disheartened teacher. "Everyone in here has detention after school today. We will sit for as long as it takes to get to the bottom of this. Class dismissed."

At the end of the school day, Ms. Beeker stood at the front of the detention hall. "This is not how I planned to spend my afternoon," Amber said to me. "Now look what your boyfriend has done! He makes me sick."

"You don't know who put those dead frog parts down the back of your pants, Amber. Don't be so quick to pick Jason. I bet it was Brent or that nasty Sean who did it."

"Well, if it wasn't Jason, I bet he put his sidekicks up to do his dirty work for him," accused Amber. "Stop defending him. He's not worth it."

"Girls, please be quiet. Remember, this is detention, not a social hour. Are any of you going to speak up and claim responsibility for what happened today, or are we going to sit here for the rest of the afternoon?" asked Ms. Beeker. She was pacing up and down the aisles, looking menacingly in Jason, Brent, and Sean's direction.

Silence continued to fill the classroom. I could tell that my classmates were growing restless as they began to wriggle in their chairs, play with their pencils, and blindly flip through the pages of their textbooks. It was becoming clearer and clearer to our teacher that no one was going to speak up. At least not today.

"Class, you leave me with no good option. I'm greatly disappointed that no one has the truthfulness to be honest about this unfortunate situation. I feel I must give you a new assignment that will be due tomorrow," declared Ms. Beeker, turning to write on the blackboard.

> PART (1): DESCRIBE IN DETAIL THE DANGERS OF LIQUID MERCURY.
> HOW COULD A VIAL OF MERCURY CAUSE AN EXPLOSION?
> PART (2): DO DISSECTED FROGS FLY?
> IF YES, DESCRIBE THIS PHENOMENON.
> IF NO, EXPLAIN HOW DEAD FROG LEGS COULD END UP DOWN A STUDENT'S PANTS.

"This paper must be typed, double-spaced, and handed in tomorrow morning, no later than nine a.m. Any student who does not meet this deadline will receive an F," she stated firmly.

With that, Ms. Beeker packed her briefcase, put her reading glasses into her shirt pocket, and left the room without another word. The class sat as still as mummies. Not one minute had passed since our angry teacher had left the detention hall before Brent got up from his seat.

"C'mon, you guys, let's ditch this place," said Brent, laughing and jabbing Sean in the arm.

"You should be thrown in a ditch, you moron!" said a disgusted Jason. "Look what you've gotten us into. Even I would not have taken the joke this far."

My friends and I gathered our books, shooting if-looks-could-kill glances in the boys' direction, and left school to begin what we believed to be our undeserved and unfair punishment essays.

* * *

CHAPTER 6
PREPARATIONS

 Today's Horoscope:

Scorpio (October 24–November 22) Set an example, and others will naturally follow. Be prepared with a few Plan B's as backups just in case you meet some troublesome complications. Tonight: You need some fun. Start thinking about the weekend.

I set my alarm clock for fifteen minutes earlier than usual. I needed the extra time for a secret visit to the garage before catching the school bus.

It was harder to wake up this morning, because I was up too late the night before finishing the time-wasting essay that Ms. Beeker had assigned in our detention hall. I have to laugh when I think of the drivel I wrote for the stupid assignment.

> *Frogs that have been dissected and pickled in formaldehyde have been known to fly out of their jars because of spontaneous combustion and extreme planetary action. The laboratory was unusually hot yesterday because Mars, the planetary troublemaker, was stirring up conflict in the universe. That made the liquid in the jar blow up, torpedoing the frog legs into the air.*

Could happen.

The garage was freezing. Now, where could Dad's toolbox be hiding? Oh, here it is, and I can't believe how few tools he has stored in his work area. There's no power saw, drill press, or even an electric sander like Marissa's father has in his workshop. What did I expect? He's a dentist, not a carpenter. Aha! Here's just the thing I need. I quickly swiped a small screwdriver and shoved it into my backpack. Will I have the guts to actually go through with my underhanded scheme?

* * *

Some time last week, I was channel surfing in an attempt to further avoid working on my Family Tree assignment, and zoned in on an old episode of *Happy Days* on TV. *Nick at Nite* was running a week long marathon of the Fonz and his friends. I was absolutely mesmerized by the gang's attempts to take apart a table at the local malt shop. The restaurant was an older version of today's Johnny Rockets chain. On the show, the Fonz was carefully loosening each screw that held up the table's legs. He did that just a little bit each day. While Ritchie and his buddies were busy talking, sipping their milkshakes and eating cheeseburgers, the Fonz was being his typical master of mischief. The gang really looked up to him, and what he did seemed so cool at the time. It worked for the *Happy Days* gang, why shouldn't it work for us Forrester girls?

* * *

Later that day during lunch, I had the opportunity to put my plan into action. But first, I had to get my friends to sign on.

"Erin, where'd you get those new earrings? They're fabulous!"

Orange feathers, which were strung through brass beads, hung from Erin's ears, practically down to her collarbone. They made a vivid contrast to her jet-black hair in its pixie hairdo and her green eyes. Erin, Amber, Marissa, and I were sitting at our usual table in the school cafeteria. We always sit together, read our horoscopes, and discuss what took place on our favorite shows the night before, who is the latest hottie, and all the other important things in our lives.

As we settled into our pizzas du jour, tuna sandwiches, and low fat yogurt, I was busy carefully pulling the screwdriver from my backpack. Three sets of eyes were focused on the tool that I was now trying to hide under the table.

"Okay, guys, this is the plan. Every Monday, we use this baby to loosen the legs on the table just a teensy bit at a time. Let's see how long it takes before the whole thing collapses."

"You've got to be kidding! Why would you want to do something so weird?" asked Amber, shaking her head in amazement.

Marissa, as usual, took my side without question. "I'm in. No matter what the reason."

"Whatever," replied Erin, who was more interested in picking the broccoli and peppers off her slice of pizza than listening to anyone else.

"I'm not usually into this sort of group statement, but if you really feel the need to do this, Jodi, I'll go along with it," said Amber hesitantly.

"Come on, it will be fun. Let's see what happens with a few spins of the screwdriver. I saw this cool episode of *Happy Days* last week on cable and I want us to copy it. It will turn out to have a really genius ending. Trust me."

After talking my friends into attempting this bizarre task, I got down to the more important business of the day—Tiffany Cooper's thirteenth birthday party, which would be held at the Regal Hotel on Saturday night.

The beautiful cream-colored invitation had arrived in the mail two months ago. It was tied in a pink satin bow and just screamed, "This is going to be an extravaganza worthy of Tiffany, who really should have been executive fashion editor of *YM* magazine, not just a common seventh grader."

The day we met, Tiffany—not Tiff, or (heaven forbid) Fany—had proclaimed, "It is too common to have a nickname." Miss Tiffy was the first preteen that any of us knew who got her very own miniature Louis Vuitton backpack. She had pictures of Jimmy Choo and Manolo Blahnik shoes taped to the inside of her locker, instead of Justin Timberlake or the Jonas Brothers, like the rest of our friends. If you wanted to be Tiffany's friend, you'd better look really good. Tiffany doesn't permit geeks into her personal space. It would be a nightmare for her to even consider looking beyond the clothes to the person underneath. Her motto is: Never leave home without your strawberry-flavored lip gloss.

"What are you wearing to Tiffany's party?" Marissa asked.

"The invitation said black tie, so I guess that means the fanciest dress I have in my closet," answered Erin.

"My mother bought me a new navy blue cocktail dress with a little matching jacket," I said. "This way, I can take the jacket off and look great for the party. All I need now are some cool strappy sandals and I'm so there!"

"I hope she puts us all at the same table and doesn't separate our group," chimed in Amber. "It might be a trip to sit with Tiffany herself, which would get us front-row seats to join in on all the action. It would be just our luck to be lumped with her nerdy little cousins or the dopey boys from the green team."

An interruption of our ideal seating plan for Tiffany's party came in the form of one smug Ms. Beeker. "I read your essay, Jodi. Quite the clever one, aren't you? I'll give you an A for your grade on the assignment when pigs fly, not frogs. Then again, at least you handed in your paper. I'm still waiting to read yours, Erin," she said, before she left in a huff.

"Don't pay her any attention," said Amber, gathering her books. "I wouldn't waste my time worrying about Ms. Beeker. Let's catch up later. Come on, we're going to be late for class."

Just then, Tiffany ran over to us and said, "I won't be in class for the rest of day. My mother arranged for an early dismissal. We have so much to do before Saturday night. You have no idea!" she gushed.

A bus had been hired by the Coopers to chauffeur the fifty-four seventh graders who'd accepted Tiffany's invitation to the Regal Hotel. Tiffany would ride in her parents' car, because she didn't want to crease the drop-dead-gorgeous, cotton candy pink dress that she would be proudly wearing. According to Tiffany, it had teensy-weensy pearl embroidery snaking its way through the folds of the designer creation. I can't even guess how much it cost.

Erin, Marissa, and Amber met at my house the day of the party, so we could get on the bus together. Fortunately, we found four seats together in the last row. From the back of the bus we could scope out all the other kids. Our little group wanted to check out who had his look together and decide who we hoped would ask us for a slow dance. Jason Kroc, my number-one pick, who would never be voted off that TV show *The Bachelorette*, was sitting next to good old Heath Berman.

Heath's parents and mine have been friends for so long that we were always thrown together at family barbecues and impromptu Sunday dinners. He is kind of cute, but is a distant second to Jason. Jason seems to grow an inch in height every time I see him at his locker. And his arms are showing some serious muscle definition these days. Oh yeah, Jason is definitely the one for me.

At the same time, Heath turned around in his seat and looked in our direction. He stood up and started walking toward the back of the bus.

"Hi, Jodi. Girls. You all look great tonight," said Heath. "Jodi, I hope that we can have one dance together at Tiffany's party," he added, with a slight blush to his face.

"Uh, yeah, sure, Heath. I'll see you later."

"Ooh, Jodi, you've been holding out on us. Why didn't you tell us that you and Heath were an item? Wait until Jason finds out. Boy, will he be jealous," kidded Erin.

"Get real, Erin. You know that there is nothing going on with Heath. He is just an old friend of the family," I said. Hmm. This could be useful. Maybe Jason will get jealous when he sees me dancing with Heath. This is going to be one interesting evening.

* * *

CHAPTER 7
TIFFANY'S PARTY

 Today's Horoscope:

Scorpio (October 24–November 22) Plans change due to a technical difficulty. Handle it with a cool head. Venus is rising and Prince Charming is waiting. Be prepared to be swept off your feet.

When I entered the ballroom, the gorgeous flowers that were suspended from the ceiling in hanging lanterns were awesome. It looked like Alice in Wonderland's garden party. Pink lilies, white tea roses, and lavender hydrangeas were dripping everywhere. People were gathering around the place card table to see where they would be seated. Next to the table was a life-sized cardboard figure of the guest of honor, Tiffany Cooper. You'd think that she was posing for an *American Idol* Tour. Souvenir pink pens were placed nearby so guests could write their compliments about Tiffany on her fake body.

If I could write what I really think about Tiff, it would be: Get over yourself, you show-off!

"Amber, you've got to see these place cards, they look just like department store credit cards!" Erin howled from clear across the entrance hallway.

"This is the best!" yelled Marissa. "I'm at the *bloomingdale's* table! Look at your place card and see if you're sitting with me."

"You are not going to believe where she stuck me!" cried Erin. "I'm at the *Loehmann's* table!"

"*Loehmann's*!" squealed Amber. "That's better than mine. I'm at *The Gap*. Where are you sitting, Jodi?"

I was too busy checking to see where Jason was sitting, and hadn't even looked for my own card yet. Oh, here it is. This cannot be real. The *Old Navy* monogrammed logo was staring up at me.

"What was Tiffany thinking when she separated all of us? I thought she really liked me."

"You? She's been calling me every day for the past few weeks to ask what color of lipstick and what shade of nail polish would match her party gown," said Marissa. "Where is Tiffany's table, anyway?"

"No surprise that she placed herself at the *Tiffany & Co.* table. How corny can you get? But look, Jason is there too! And all the best-dressed kids in class are sitting with them," said Amber.

"That figures," agreed Erin.

I was only too happy to go in search of the girls' restroom, to calm down and to adjust the spaghetti straps of my new blue dress that kept slipping down. I opened the door to the first toilet stall and gasped. There were lavender lilies floating in the toilet bowl.

Should I go to the bathroom or take a picture?

This has to be some sort of mistake. I opened the next stall, and there was another lily gliding across the water, just begging to be flushed. Was this some kind of joke, or had Tiffany's parents lost their minds trying to impress the guests?

The way I was feeling about not being placed with my girl friends or with Jason, combined with the embarrassment of sitting at the *Old Navy* table, drove me to a flushing frenzy. One stall was occupied, but I managed to make all the other lilies that I could find disappear in record time. I adjusted my straps, brushed my hair, applied a fresh coat of watermelon lip gloss, and was ready to meet my tablemates.

What a bratty thing to do. I feel kind of horrible about my temper tantrum. I have to keep it together.

Closing the door to the restroom, I made my way to the *Old Navy* table, passing *Saks Fifth Avenue, Sports Authority, Abercrombie & Fitch, Prada*, and *Neiman Marcus*. I didn't dare look for too long, fearing someone would notice and ask me where I was sitting. I could not handle any further humiliation. I noticed little porcelain shopping bags were positioned in front of every place setting. Tiffany's name and her birth date, September 24, 1995, were inscribed on the bags in a beautiful shade of raspberry. Chocolate mints in the shape of miniature shoes and handbags were carefully arranged in a teensy-weensy glass department store case. Pink and cream embroidered tablecloths, matching lace-trimmed cloth napkins, and a humongous floral centerpiece completed the picture.

When I arrived at my table, all my fears were realized. The only friendly face I saw was that of my old pal, Heath.

"Jodi! Over here! I've saved you a place next to me!" said Heath enthusiastically.

"Oh. Hi, Heath. Thanks a lot," I said halfheartedly, as I sank down onto the smooth, pink satin-covered chair, almost slipping right onto the floor.

The smells of the sickeningly sweet star lilies and the overflowing selection of chocolates were starting to make me feel nauseous. As the band loudly belted out, "I'm coming out, I want the world to know that Tiffany loves you so…," the guest of honor appeared in a slowly rising pink cloud of artificial mist.

"Ugh. This is going to kill me, Heath. I truly don't think I can take much more of this ridiculousness."

All of a sudden, the band started playing Kelly Clarkson's hit "*A Moment Like This*." I got excited, expecting Jason to approach and ask me to dance. Instead, he draped his arm over Tiffany's shoulder as he led her out onto the dance floor. Rats!

"Who do they think they are? The king and queen of the prom?"

"You're not jealous, are you, Jodi?" asked Heath.

Dejected, I slumped down in my seat and mumbled, "This wasn't the way it was supposed to turn out. Where's my Prince Charming? My horoscope said he'd be waiting!"

"Come on, Jodi, let's dance. It'll be fun," Heath said, as he tapped me on the shoulder and startled me into reality. Reluctantly, I joined Heath as the band began to play their rendition of "Celebrate". While dancing, I started to feel sticky and sweaty.

Maybe I'm coming down with the flu. It's been going around.

The mist, which should have been long gone by this point, was slowly rising, thickening and filling the room. Sleek hairdos were starting to frizz up. Huge beads of perspiration were saturating the men's tuxedo shirt collars. The women were fanning themselves with their hands and drying their wet foreheads with the beautiful lace napkins. Not only was the mist rising, but it was becoming so dense that I could no longer see my table, which was only a few feet from the dance floor.

I heard Tiffany yell to Mrs. Cooper, "Tell someone to turn off that stupid mist machine! Now!"

"I can't breathe! I need some air!"

"Get off! You're stepping on my dress!"

"Stop bumping into me! What is happening?"

"Quick, where's the emergency exit?"

These were some of the cries I heard from the guests in the crowded, foggy room.

I was still standing on the dance floor, though feeling somewhat paralyzed. Heath reached for my hand and said, "Jodi, I'm right here. Please grab my hand. Don't be afraid, I'll get us out of here."

To my surprise, his touch made the weird scene seem a little less confusing.

"Attention! Attention, please! Nobody panic," exclaimed Mr. Cooper through the microphone. "Everything's fine, stay where you are. We have opened all the doors. It's just a minor mechanical breakdown. The room will be cleared up in just a few minutes. Please don't run anywhere!"

* * *

Many of the guests had already located emergency exit doors and had found breathing room in the fresh air outside. Many of the adults were laughing about the major misty mess, but the girls found nothing to laugh about and ran to the bathroom. Some were kneeling in front of the hand dryers, desperately trying to erase the sweat from under their arms, while others were drying their limp hair.

Tiffany had run into the bathroom and almost fainted when she looked in the mirror. "Oh, #%&!#@*&%#@#&*!" Her high-pitched shriek could be heard through the door and down the hall. At the beginning of the party, her face, arms, shoulders, and back were a perfect bronze shade (thanks to her fake tanning cream), but were now a checkerboard of brown and beige blotches. She looked more like someone who suffered from a strange tropical skin disease than a prom queen wannabee.

While many of the girls were in the restroom, Jason and a couple of his buddies were busy drifting from table to table through the pink steamy haze. The unsuspecting adults didn't see the boys sneaking sips from wine and martini glasses. The kids were having a grand time polishing off the vodka and the red, white, and pink wine in the glasses that were on the adults' tables. Later, the waiters would be surprised to find that all the glasses looked like they had already been put through the dishwasher.

By the time the murky pink fog cleared, I was thrilled and relieved to meet up with Erin, Amber, and Marissa. They started snickering about the perfect Tiffany, who was now looking wilted, blotchy, and utterly annoyed.

I popped a half-melted chocolate shoe into my mouth and quietly said to Amber, "This couldn't happen to a nicer person."

"Come on, guys, do we have to stick it out till twelve thirty tonight? I really don't think I'll make it!" begged Amber, obviously hoping we could all just leave and get a pizza somewhere.

"Oh, Amber, get over it. This party is just getting started. We don't want to miss a thing. I mean, everyone is going to be talking about this scene for months. If we don't stay, we'll be totally out of it!" pleaded Marissa.

"What's come over you, Marissa? Who cares if we miss any more of the big show-off's performance? I want to go home," said Amber. Pulling out her colorful cell phone, she announced, "I'm calling my folks. Who's coming with me?"

"I'm staying." I spoke up. "Even though I think Tiffany is shallow and only interested in material things, I'm starting to feel sorry for her tonight. I wouldn't want something like this to happen to me. She's been dreaming about this party for so long, and look how horrible it's turning out. Let's go find her and say something to make her feel better."

Amber was set on leaving, but Marissa and Erin stayed on with me. Fortunately for the Coopers, the crowd settled down and enjoyed the dinner, dancing, and fabulous selection of party games. Mr. Cooper delivered a lovely speech in honor of his daughter's birthday. The band continued to play and no other catastrophes occurred. Around midnight, the guests were slowly getting their coats and calling for their cars.

"Jason hasn't looked at me the whole night," I confided to Marissa.

"There he is, standing over by the bathroom. Here's your chance to say something to him," Marissa said, giving me a gentle shove in Jason's direction.

"Okay. I'll go over to say good-bye."

As I got closer to Jason, I noticed something rather peculiar about his behavior. He seemed unsteady on his feet, and I heard him slurring his words.

Just as I started to say, "Jason, I want...," he turned in my direction and threw up what seemed like his entire chicken nugget dinner, all over my beautiful blue strappy sandals.

"You're so disgusting! How gross can you get?" I screamed, running away from him as fast as I could. I lunged into the girls' bathroom, which had now become my second home.

I immediately slipped off my once-beautiful sandals and began to cry. There were chunks of what looked like partially chewed chicken and French fries, gnawed carrot sticks, and strawberry marshmallow pie coating my toes.

This can't be happening to me. Why didn't my horoscope warn me? I would have just stayed home tonight.

By the time Dad and Mom were scheduled to pick me up, I had successfully washed off most of the undigested food from my sandals, and the stench of vomit had almost disappeared. I grabbed one of the party favors that were sitting on the table near the exit. Naturally, it was a cardboard copy of an original blue and white *Tiffany* box. It was filled with a sugary, gooey slice of Tiffany's pink birthday cake.

"I swear, my bat mitzvah party will be nothing like this!" I cried. I dumped the cake into the nearest garbage can.

I saw my parents waiting in our car outside the hotel. They took one glance at the pathetic expression on my face and knew better than to ask me any questions about the evening. The Milner family drove home in silence.

* * *

CHAPTER 8
TEETH AND TALES

 Today's Horoscope:

Scorpio (October 24–November 22) You will be in the right place at the wrong time. Beware of strangers bearing tall tales. Your sense of direction and ability to sort through what is unfathomable for many comes to light.

After a tough weekend, I looked forward to getting back to school and my Monday morning routine. I wonder how many more turns of the screw it will take before something really interesting happens to our lunchroom table. I can't wait to get my Family Tree assignment over with. It's taking too much of my time, and there is something strangely disturbing about the whole project. Marissa is not the only one having trouble with it.

"Girls, don't forget that I'll be picking you both up after school today when the volleyball game is over," Mom said over breakfast.

"Please try to come early, Mom. I'd love for you to see me in action against the Roslyn Raiders," Becky said. "Their school took the girls' state championship for the last two years in a row, and our team has a very good chance of beating them. I can already picture us grabbing the trophy from their hot, sweaty hands."

"I'll try my best to get there as early as I can, but I'm sub-bing today at a private school on the other side of town. You know that I'm usually there for all of your games, but it may be a bit tight today," said Mom.

"At least I'll be there for you, Becky. My friends and I are looking forward to cheering on your team. We'll walk over to the high school at the end of school."

"Great. See you later," said Becky.

The two of us took off in different directions to catch the bus that would take us to our respective schools.

The buzz among my friends at Forrester Middle School was centered on Tiffany's party. Jason and his friends were the butt of many jokes because of their dumb drinking di-saster. In fact, Jason was still looking a bit blue around the gills and this time it had nothing to do with his team color. Rumor had it that those jerks had been grounded for two weeks. Let's see them come up with a plan to weasel out of this one!

The day seemed to drag on and on, but I couldn't wait to watch Becky play in what was sure to be a tight game. The gossip was that the Roslyn Raiders had all kinds of tricks and sleek, yet legal maneuvers that were pre-planned to catch their opponents off guard. This was apparently how they had taken the championship last year. But Becky's volleyball coach, Mr. Stevenson, was secretly working on his own complex pass-ing combinations. He was certain that his counterattack would baffle any high school team. He wanted that trophy, and today was the day to prove that his team had what it would take to be number one in the district.

By the time I arrived at the high school gym with my friends, the scoreboard showed that the Raiders were already leading 6-2. I could see that Becky was looking frustrated but determined, and ready to spike the ball across the net at any moment. One of her teammates served the ball. The opposing team's tallest player quickly returned it. Becky jumped to receive the ball that was set up behind her, and punched the volleyball back over the net into an open space. Score one for the Forrester girls! This was the spark the team needed to get on the winning track.

"Way to go, Becky!" cheered Amber. "Jodi, your sister is really good."

It really made me feel proud when Amber said that to me.

Another serve was delivered to the Raiders. Their star athlete dove to get her hand under the regulation white volleyball before it hit the floor. Her timing was a bit off because the ball smashed into the floor anyway. Another point for Forrester! Cheers from the sidelines broke out as the scoreboard clicked 6-4.

The home team girl served again, but this time it was returned with a crushing blow to the far left corner of the court. No one even saw it coming.

The ball went back to the Raiders for a new serve. A menacing member of the champion team tossed the ball with one hand and then quickly socked it with the other. As the volleyball was propelled through the air, Becky and Lonni Browne, another forward, leaped into the air at the same time. The collision of the girls' heads was loud enough for us to hear from the bleachers, and both girls went down.

The referee blew his whistle to signal a stop in the action.

"Oh, no! I think my sister is hurt. I have to get down there."
I sprinted over the seats to get to Becky as fast as possible,
jumping over books, backpacks, and laptops.

When I reached Becky, I was so relieved to see that she
and Lonni were already sitting up and talking to Coach Stevenson. They seemed fine, except for Lonni's bruised forehead
and Becky's bloody mouth. Their bright purple and white uni-
forms were splattered with red specks, evidence of the midair
crash.

Mom walked into the gym at that moment and stared in
horror at the blood oozing from her eldest daughter's mouth.
She ran to Becky's side, where I was holding my sister's hand.
Checking for damage, Mom saw that the injury was not as serious as she had first thought.

"Looks like you girls might have some headaches and
sport black-and-blue shiners tomorrow. Take these ice packs
and keep them on for fifteen minutes before coming back on
the court," barked Coach Stevenson. "Mrs. Milner, maybe you
should have Dr. Milner look at Becky's teeth later tonight."

"I'm not waiting until tonight. We're going to my husband's
office right now. You'll have to replace Becky for the remainder
of the game. Good luck. Come on, kids, we're out of here,"
said Mom.

"Please, Mom, I don't want to leave. I swear, I'm fine. I
don't want to go to Dad's office. Let me stay and finish out the
game," pleaded Becky. "I have to help my team win."

At that moment, the referee blew his whistle, signaling that
play was to begin again. The Forrester girls rushed back on the
court and Becky was getting ready to join them.

"This is not open for discussion. I'm getting the car. Jodi, get your sister's things and call Dad on my cell phone to let him know that we are on our way over," ordered Mom.

"If it turns out that this is just a big waste of time and my team loses, you'll owe me big-time!" said an infuriated Becky.

Fifteen frantic minutes of driving later, we arrived at the dental office. Dragging a blood-stained and exasperated teenager by the hand, Mom barged into Dad's examining room.

"Jodi, sit in the waiting room. I'm not sure how long this is going to take," said Mom, disappearing behind the closed door.

I plopped into one of my favorite oversized armchairs in Dad's waiting room and took out my homework binder. I have been coming to this office since I was born. Most people don't like the medicinal smell of a dentist's office, but it was familiar to me and not at all scary. Because I've never had a cavity in my whole life, the sound of the drill didn't spook me either.

Lots of magazines were on the wall rack across from the front door. *Highlights for Children* had always been one of our family's favorites, but there was something for everyone's reading taste: *People* magazine, *Sports Illustrated*, *Newsweek*, *Architectural Digest*, *Men's Health*, *Ladies Home Journal*, *YM*, and even a magazine for yoga lovers. A water cooler with small paper cones sat in one corner of the waiting room, and a table for little kids covered with blocks, wooden jigsaw puzzles, and board books was in another corner. One wall was actually a full-length window that looked out into a beautiful Japanese garden. There was even a small pond and waterfall. With winter approaching, the garden was not looking as beautiful as it had in the spring and summer, but the cold running water was glistening in the afternoon sun.

As I worked on my math homework, I felt someone eyeballing me suspiciously. Funny, I hadn't even noticed him when I first sat down. Was it because of all the excitement over Becky's injury? Or because the odd stranger was sitting in a shadowed corner of the room?

"Are you the one?" asked Ned Biggins, in a voice no louder than a faint whisper.

"The one what?" I said, confused.

"Uh…nothing. What I meant to say is that you're the spitting image of your mother's picture that's hanging in Doc's office. I'm Ned Biggins, and I've been your dad's patient since before your big sister was born. And by the way, that was her, right? What happened to her pretty face today?" he asked. "I hope the other guy looks worse!"

"Wait, go back to what you said before. Why am I the one?" I asked again.

"Never you mind. It's a private matter between your father and me," he winked.

I couldn't help but notice this odd man's clothes. As I looked him over more carefully, I spotted old black tennis shoes and white socks on his feet, a wrinkled gray suit, and a red and green plaid bowtie clipped to the collar of his dingy white shirt. The only time my father's friends wore bowties was with tuxedos, and then they were usually solid black. Mr. Biggins looked like he needed a shave, and his glasses were tinted a light yellow tone, giving his face a somewhat pasty appearance.

He also wore an old baseball cap with the Giants logo embroidered on it.

Because I was so busy sizing up this weird guy, I did not hear the examining room door open. It caught me by surprise when the dental assistant said, "Hi, guys." The shock made me drop all the pages of my homework folder and they scattered everywhere, even under Mr. Biggins' feet. As I leaped to pick up the loose papers, Mr. Biggins leaned over and handed me the papers that had drifted in his direction. At that moment, I got an unasked for and undesired close-up of his mouth.

"Here, m'lady, I think these are yours," he hissed, breathing out a stream of air that smelled like cigarettes and rotten eggs.

Boy, I hope Dad wears his face mask tight enough not to breathe in this joker's smelly breath. Peeuuww.

* * *

Dad entered the waiting room with his arms draped over Mom's and Becky's shoulders and announced, "Good news! Becky will be fine. It was only a superficial injury to her gum that didn't require any stitches," he said. "Becky, you're going to have to keep an ice pack on and off your cheek for the rest of the evening, to prevent swelling," he continued. "See you all later at dinner. Sharon, I think Becky will need something easy to swallow tonight. How about if I pick up some fish chowder at *Mac's* on my way home?" Turning to his scruffy old patient, he said, "Ned, so sorry to keep you waiting. You know how kids are these days. Please come in."

On the drive home, Becky whipped out her cell phone and called her team captain to find out the final score between the Falcons and the Raiders. After a brief update, she flipped the cell closed with disgust.

"I can't stand it, Mom! We lost, ten to four. My team didn't score again after I left. This is all your fault! I didn't even need stitches. The girls were counting on me. They really needed me! How could you have done this to me? How am I going to face them tomorrow?" cried Becky. The ice pack was now melting and dripping over her already stained uniform.

"Becky, dear, it was the right thing to do. It was for your own good. You could have had a serious problem," comforted Mom.

"I'm so tired of you treating me like a baby. I'm almost ready for college, you know, and then I'll be on my own, with no one to boss me around," said Becky defiantly. "You could at least say you're sorry my team lost. We really needed this win. Coach Stevenson was hoping that this win would give us a chance at district."

"I think I've had enough of your disrespect, young lady," remarked Mom.

Before she completed her thought, I interrupted. "Becky, I really feel for you. You definitely would have made the difference in the final score. You were playing so great today. But I have to ask Mom a question. Do you know who that strange-looking man was in Dad's waiting room? He said he had a private matter with Daddy that I think had something to do with me. He gave me the creeps."

"Don't pay any attention to him," Mom said, but she didn't answer me right away. She suddenly seemed so weird. "That's just Mr. Biggins. Years ago, he handled what seemed like a simple business matter for Dad, which unfortunately got rather complicated. But that's in the past. Don't give him a second thought. He's a bit of a weirdo and is always telling tall tales." Maybe, it was my imagination, but there was something in her voice that left me feeling rather freaked.

* * *

CHAPTER 9
SAFARI

 Today's Horoscope:

Scorpio (October 24–November 22) Hopes are high and they will be fulfilled. Something special awaits you. Reach out to others and make a difference with some of your friends.
Tonight: You have permission to see the sunrise.

In the car, Mom turned to me and asked, "What did you think of the service in Temple Beth Or? Did Jason perform like the superstar that you think he is? Or are you still mad at him for throwing up on your beautiful blue sandals at Tiffany's party?"

"Oh, Mom, I am so over that. I still think he's the coolest. He did great. He read from the Torah as if he were a junior rabbi. I didn't realize that he knew Hebrew so well. I just thought he was a cutup in Hebrew School like the rest of his jerky friends."

"She's right, Mrs. Milner," said Marissa. "I never had any Hebrew lessons because I've been brought up Catholic, but it sounded like he breezed right through his part in the ceremony. His speech, thanking his parents, teachers and rabbi, was also right on."

"It was amazing that the boys who usually can't wait to jam into their seats way in the back row of the chapel were sitting way up front and were actually quiet while Jason was up on the bimah. I've never seen anything like it. He's like a movie star. He looked so handsome in his new navy blue suit. Am I gushing too much?"

"Okay, I get the picture. I hope the party lives up to your high expectations. Barry, make that left on Pine Street to avoid the traffic," directed Mom. "Girls, take notes on the big bash, I want to hear all the details when we pick you up later."

As our car approached the Hotel Le Grande, Mom turned to Marissa and me and said, "Dad and I will pick you up at twelve thirty. Have a great time."

When Dad slowed down to let us out at the curb, we were met with a shocking surprise. We expected to see the usual luxurious entrance of the regal old hotel. Instead, thick vines were entwined in the overhang to the lobby, and hanging coconuts and fake monkeys added extra startling touches. The valet who greeted us to the Kroc Bar Mitzvah was dressed in khakis, sported a pith helmet that seemed too small for his head, and wore un-scuffed jungle boots on his feet. If that wasn't enough to catch our attention, he had a live crocodile on a leash.

"Allow me to escort you to the safari in the main ballroom, young ladies," he said, giving a low bow.

"Marissa, close your mouth. Come on, let's get going. If this is the beginning of Jason's party, can you imagine how the rest of it is going to be? I can't wait!"

We waved goodbye to Dad and Mom, who were trying to stifle their laughter at the spectacle before them.

The jungle theme didn't stop there. The sound of pounding drums and the cawing of parrots drew us to the hors d'oeuvres stations. In one corner of the vast room, a man who could have been Tarzan's lost twin brother was carving a gigantic turkey breast. Mixed in the crowd were several young waitresses wearing grass skirts, bright yellow tube tops, and had multicolored leis hung around their necks. It was their job to serve the pigs in blankets, coconut chicken on skewers, fried cheese sticks, mini pizzas, steak sandwiches, and other yummy finger foods.

After stuffing our faces with everything that was handed us by the hula girls, we and many of the other guests made our way to the sushi station in the far corner. There, the servers were dressed in white karate robes and wore tall chef hats.

Before reaching the sushi bar, we had to pass the "Vodka Slide."

Stopping in her tracks and almost crashing into Marissa, Amber exclaimed, "You must be kidding! What in the world is this setup?"

"Shh, Amber. Get a grip. Haven't you ever seen a martini slide before? I saw one just last month when I went with my parents to my Cousin Valerie's wedding in New York City. It's the latest attraction for adults," explained the suddenly sophisticated-sounding Marissa.

Before us was a four-foot-high ice sculpture sitting on a huge table. The sculpture was in the shape of an elephant with a huge tusk. Instead of water flowing into the glasses, vodka was pouring into martini glasses that were placed strategically under the animal's snout. Russian vodka was substituted for ordinary tap water. The whole setup was very colorful because the alcohol was in different flavors, to suit the guests' tastes. Little dishes of olives, onions, lemon and lime wedges, and orange peels were on the table for the adults to plop into their glasses. We kept walking.

Arriving at the sushi station, we grabbed the tiny raw fish bits, which were covered with black seaweed and white rice. While maneuvering our chopsticks with little success, pieces of cucumber, rice, and tuna kept dropping on the floral carpet beneath our feet. It was starting to get extremely messy and crunchy down there.

"I'm surprised we haven't spotted Tiffany yet," said Erin. "I bet she's probably in the ladies' room applying another layer of her shiny Angel's Breath lip gloss."

"How obnoxious is this, Jodi?" asked Amber, as she was stuffing a lamb chop into her mouth. Grabbing another one from the shirtless waiter who was wearing a giant headdress, she mumbled, "I wonder where we are sitting this time? It couldn't be worse than Tiffany's seating chart."

We wandered back to the main entrance to find the place card table. Erin ran ahead as if she were in a 5K and began searching for our names. It took a while because the place cards weren't in the form of the usual paper notes, but were actually plastic crocodile key chains. It wasn't easy to find them, since they were suspended on the same type of hanging jungle vines that greeted us at the hotel entrance. Erin practically had to jump up and yank down each chain. Our names were written on the crocodiles' stomachs, and "Jason Kroc's Bar Mitzvah— October 19, 2007." Decorated the animal's back. This time, we all found ourselves at Table #6.

"Whew, at least we are all sitting together," I said. "Look, the tables are carrying the jungle theme even further." In the center of the dark green tablecloths sat rattan cages in a bed of moss and wild orchids.

"Maybe I'm imagining it, but something seems to be moving inside our centerpiece," whispered Marissa.

Amber leaned closer to the cage and cried out, "You're right! There are live lizards crawling inside! I can't believe this!"

At this point, I was still unfazed by the wild displays of silliness. I had only one concern. "Does anyone know where Jason is sitting? By the way, has anyone even seen Jason yet?"

In unison, we scanned the room. We didn't have to look far, because Jason's buddies were all sitting together at Table #1, and it was a good guess that the bar mitzvah boy would be joining them soon.

Fortunately, Tiffany was spotted sitting at Table #4 with the TLC's (Three Lame Chicks) from the junior varsity cheerleading squad. Her rose-colored satin mini dress didn't match the jungle decor, but she could have been mistaken for a pink flamingo as she stretched her neck looking for Jason.

"The bad news is, we're not sitting with Jason; but, the good news is, we're not sitting with Tiffany," I laughed.

At that moment, the lights flickered and the deejay asked everyone to take seats in the main ballroom. As the guests settled down, the room got even darker. Three large, bald men wearing long grass skirts suddenly appeared and began banging thunderously on the o drums between their legs. In a flash, a fire dancer leaped into the center of the room and threw himself into a rhythmic jungle dance. He twirled a flaming hoop over his head, barely missing the crystal chandelier above. After an amazing demonstration of his fire-eating skills, the room was hushed. The dead silence was broken by the emcee announcing, "Heeeeeeeeeeeeeeere's Jason!"

Four men dressed in safari garb carried Jason into the ballroom. He was lounging comfortably on a bamboo platform, held high above their heads. The guides lowered the chaise and Jason jumped off, narrowly missing tripping over one of the guide's fake elephant rifles. Just when I thought it couldn't get any more ridiculous, Jason ran through the burning hoop of fire to complete his grand entrance.

The applause that followed this opening act was deafening. While the guests were still applauding Jason's daring feat, Erin turned to me and said in disgust, "And this is the boy that you've been dreaming about?"

"Isn't he incredible?"

"Yeah, right, incredibly stupid," answered Erin.

Later, as the adults were being served their main course, the emcee's job was to entertain the teenagers. He handed out navy blue T-shirts to all the kids. The boys immediately stripped off their jackets and dress shirts to put on their souvenir T-shirts. Only some of the girls bothered putting them on over their gowns, because the others were afraid of ruining their makeup and hairstyles. On the back of the tees in large, bright, bold yellow letters was: The Kroc Rocks.

When everyone was properly dressed, the emcee signaled to the band to start the Coke/Pepsi game. A line of eager girls took their positions on one side of the dance floor, facing an opposite line of Jason and his male friends.

"Coke!" yelled the bandleader.

I ran with Amber and Erin to sit on the boys' knees, which is how the game is played. Marissa could not help but notice that half the boys were missing. It seemed that the word "Coke" was a pre-planned signal for some of Jason's buddies to open the centerpiece cages and let the lizards run wild. Jason was laughing so hard that he didn't notice Tiffany racing toward him to stake out her claim to his knees. The impact of Tiffany landing on him threw him off balance. The two of them tumbled backward, landing flat on their backs in the middle of the dance floor. Tiffany looked horrified, because her poofy dress twisted around and exposed her pink panties. Jason was too interested in the iguanas that were crawling across the guests' dinner plates to notice Tiffany's embarrassment.

Mr. Kroc jumped up from his seat, grabbed the microphone from the emcee, and said, "Okay, everybody. If you're lucky enough to catch an iguana or other crawling creature, you will get to take home the centerpiece."

Laughing, the emcee took back the microphone and announced, "Come on, boys and girls join me on the dance floor. We have more games and music in store for you. How about we quiet things down and make the next dance a lady's choice?"

I thought that this was my chance to finally get Jason alone, but Tiffany had smoothed down her cocktail dress and already made a beeline for Jason. The blonde bimbette almost knocked him over again in her rush to ask the guest of honor to dance. I stopped shooting daggers at Tiffany when Heath tapped me on the shoulder.

"I know this is a lady's choice, Jodi, but I'd like to dance this one with you," said Heath.

Okay, knowing I had clearly missed my opportunity to dance with Jason, I said to myself, "Why not?"

After what seemed like hours more of listening to the old song "Crocodile Rock," rapping gorillas, hip-hopping hyenas, pop-rock panthers, and watching Jason's foolish attempt at juggling bananas and coconuts, I finally came to a new conclusion.

What a jerk! Maybe I've been missing something all along. I definitely must re-chart my romantic destiny. I'm out of here.

As I went to say good-bye to Jason, he leaned forward to give me a kiss on the cheek. His breath reminded me of burnt toast. Looking closer at his face, I saw that his eyebrows were singed from the flaming hoop that he had jumped through earlier.

Yup, I think he's history, I thought sadly to myself. *Marissa and I must make time very soon to re-plot my star chart. I can't understand why Jason and I are having so many problems getting together. All signals were pointing that we would be girlfriend and boyfriend. I am not happy.*

* * *

CHAPTER 10
CAFETERIA LUNCH

 Today's Horoscope:

Capricorn (December 22–January 19) November's full moon is peaking in your sign, stirring up your moods, desires, and relationships. It's likely your life will suddenly take an unexpected change in direction. Whatever twists arise in the road ahead, you shouldn't let them worry you. Your date with fate is simply rearranging the position of your life. Go for it!

Becky was the first one down to the breakfast table Monday morning. She opened the *Forrester Tribune* and looked at me with a mischievous grin as she read her own horoscope aloud.

"Gee, Jodes, I think that maybe there is something to this crazy astrology stuff. I like this one! Now, let's see, what's going to happen in your world today? How right on are these forecasts? Ouch!"

I gave Becky a soft punch in the shoulder in response to this sarcastic remark, but was still wondering what the stars had in store for me that day. "So, what does it say already?"

Clearing her throat as if to accept an MTV award, Becky read: "'Be more upbeat when a friend comes forward to share. Join friends and enjoy. You might be a lot friendlier than you have been in awhile. Well, Jodi, sounds like you are going to make some new friends, huh? You could use some!" said Becky, as she flipped her bangs out of her eyes.

"Leave me alone! Mom, can you make her stop?" I begged, as Becky kept jabbing me in the ribs.

What I didn't say, aloud, was that I was very troubled about the morning's horoscope reading. Becky's horoscope should have been mine. *I am the one that needs a "date with fate," not my superstar sister. I mean, Becky already thinks she should be wearing a crown.*

Later that Monday, October 21, Erin, Marissa, Amber, and I met at our usual cafeteria lunch table right on schedule. We relived the gruesome events of Jason's bar mitzvah on Saturday night.

"So, Jodi, are you still in love with the doofus of the year?" asked Marissa.

"Jason is not a doofus. Would you just cut him some slack!" I still felt like I had to defend him.

"You've got to be kidding! Why do you always stick up for that jerk? He acted like a complete fool at Tiffany's party and at his own bar mitzvah. He should have been embarrassed to death, but instead he acted like king of the jungle, or should I say ape-man? If you're still hot for him, you can have him! I'd have sent him packing months ago," declared Marissa.

As far as Marissa, Erin, and Amber were concerned, Jason had lost his babe-magnet status and was now considered just another loser. My three friends started scanning the room to see who they could nominate to be the next object of their intense like.

"Will you all just be quiet a minute and listen?" I asked. "After going to Tiffany's bungled bash and Jason's jungle bar mitzvah, I decided to make some changes for my own party. I'd really appreciate just five minutes of your time. Please?"

The girls reluctantly sat back in their chairs, and while munching the final morsels of their lunches, turned their eyes and ears to me.

"I have been thinking about moving my bat mitzvah to that beautiful place on the Jersey shore. You know, the Spinnaker House, where my family has Sunday brunch every summer. My mom was telling me that it was just renovated and has a very upbeat feeling now. They built this huge deck that goes out over the water. It should look awesome in the winter.

"My dad suggested renting a bus big enough to take all my friends down to the shore, if this idea works out. The bus, which will be waiting outside the synagogue, caters to parties. I heard it has TVs, CD players, radio, a DVD, and even a bar! Don't look at me that way; I'm not talking about beer and alcoholic stuff. I'm talking about free sodas and all kinds of great snacks. You know, the works. Becky has a friend who makes the best party CDs, and she promised she'd have him burn my favorite songs—so we'd have music enough for the entire ride. We'd be partying before we even got down to the shore!"

"Jodi, slow down. Breathe. You look like you might explode. That sounds pretty expensive, and you haven't even told us about the actual party. I thought you were disgusted by how much money Tiffany and Jason's families blew on their kids' parties. I'm confused," said Amber.

"I know it'd be expensive, but it won't look as overdone as theirs. I mean, I'm not even considering carving stations or a sushi bar during the hors d'oeuvres hour."

"Do you mean to tell us that your bat mitzvah is in two months and you still don't have a place reserved for the party?" asked an amazed Marissa.

"Don't get all bent out of shape, Marissa. We still have the synagogue reserved for the reception, but I was thinking of something more exciting. Here's the rest of my plan."

I felt wound up as I said, "Hear me out. I've really thought about how I can make the room look totally drop-dead inspirational. The place cards will be tarot cards, and the table numbers will be floating inside crystal balls. The centerpieces will be incense holders. There will be a large selection of different incense sticks at each table, so that the guests can choose their favorite scent. And get this, I was thinking of having a psychic, a handwriting analyst, a palm reader, and a tea leaf reader during the cocktail hour. It'll be such a cosmic event! I don't think I've ever heard of anyone having this theme at a bar or bar mitzvah before. I might even start a new trend!"

"Wait a minute, Jodi," said Marissa, exasperated. "You are surely not expecting your parents to approve of such a spectacle! Are you?"

"Well, yeah. I mean, they know how into this I am. They've heard my music, they've seen my room, and they've smelled my candles and incense. It's me. It's who I am. How can they reject it? They'd be rejecting me! Jodi the Scorpio. It's the symbol of me—who I am and who I will always be!"

Just as I was trying to further defend myself, Tiffany sashayed over to our table and sat down, uninvited.

"Hey, you guys, is this a p-r-i-v-a-t-e conference?" she asked in an exaggerated whisper. Tiffany had this habit of spelling words when she thought that she was onto something special. "You all look like you're telling ghost stories. What's up?" asked a curious Tiffany, staring directly into my eyes.

I was seriously hoping that by the time my bat mitzvah arrived, Tiffany would have left town for some foreign country. I really did not want to put the pink diva on my guest list.

"No, Tiffany, we were not telling ghost stories, we have more important matters to discuss," blurted Erin, without a clue as to what she would say next.

Bringing the conversation back to herself, Tiffany asked, with a triumphant look on her snotty face, "Jodi, did you happen to notice that your *boyfriend* Jason asked me to be his partner for every slow dance at his party?"

"He's not my boyfriend now, he never was, and personally I think he's a creep. You can keep him," I answered, trying to save face. "I'm so over him. Lots-a-luck."

Just then, my friends heard a low creaking noise. They began to feel tremors as if an earthquake had hit Forrester Middle School, except no one else in the lunchroom seemed to notice. Before Tiffany could say another obnoxious word, Erin's milk carton began to topple over, and all the silverware on Amber and Marissa's side of the table slowly edged its way to the corner where smug looking Tiffany was sitting.

We looked at each other as the noise grew louder, smiled knowingly, and hurriedly pushed our chairs back. We realized that the time had come. Tiffany was still babbling on about Jason, and was not paying attention to the rocking motion of the old wooden lunch table.

The unsuspecting Tiffany had no idea what was about to happen, but within seconds she was covered with the remains of my strawberry yogurt, Erin's cheeseburger, Amber's tuna pita sandwich, and Marissa's mustard-cove dog.

A loud crash stunned the rest of the fourth period cafeteria students and staff into silence. The loosened screws that were barely holding our table together finally popped out and sent the legs flying.

This moment of silence was fleeting as the vice principal, Mr. Sandalwood, came running over to where the commotion was occurring. He looked in horror at Tiffany's stained and splattered outfit. "Miss Cooper, are you alright? What happened here? This is a disaster! What did you do to yourself?" he shouted.

Tiffany started crying. "I don't think I'm hurt, but my favorite suede pants are ruined forever. These horrible girls must have had something to do with it!" she said, pointing her finger at me and my friends. "I knew they hated me," Tiffany sobbed, as she wiped her nose on her already dirty sleeve.

"Please, Tiffany, don't accuse your friends," said Mr. Sandalwood. "It's not their fault that these old tables have started to fall apart. It's a miracle that no one was seriously hurt. Fortunately, new aluminum tables have already been ordered and should arrive next week. Please accompany me to the nurse's office so Miss Hackleberry can check you over for any injury. She'll help you clean up the mess on your clothes.

The rest of you kids go find another table until the fifth period bell rings."

By this time, every student was staring in the direction of what would soon be referred to as the "Tiffany Table Topple." Quiet laughter, and debates of how such a thing could have happened. Could it have been done on purpose? If so, by whom? And how? One student was already taking bets. The whispering was running through the crowd like wind through a hollow tunnel. It certainly made this cafeteria period the most memorable of the year so far.

As Tiffany left with Mr. Sandalwood, she turned around to give a final sneer in our direction. However, she was having a hard time keeping up with him while picking the scraps of food from her now stained and grubby pants. My stomach was starting to hurt; I was trying as hard as I could to keep in the laughter that was welling up inside me from exploding.

Thinking back to the day when I borrowed Dad's screwdriver, I never imagined what the end result would be. When I get home from school today, I have to remember to get rid of the evidence, namely the guilty tool. Would the Fonz have been proud of me? I had a sinking feeling that I deserved a lecture on crossing the line.

Getting rid of the evidence would have to wait, because Marissa and I had a four thirty p.m. appointment with Madame Shumsky, another one of our favorite online psychics. Unlike Scarlet Skye, The Madame was famous for her ability to predict which couples were made for each other. She had the best site for charting romantic destinies. Obviously, Jason, who was a Libra, was not balancing with my Scorpio sign.

Even though it looks like Jason and my "like affair" is headed straight to the recycling bin, I wanted to give us one more chance. The bell rang, alerting me that it was time to go to science lab.

* * *

CHAPTER 11
ROMANTIC DESTINY

"Hi. Mom. School was really interesting today. There was a major accident in the lunchroom. Don't worry, no one got hurt. A table collapsed and spilled food all over Tiffany's new cream-colored pants. But that was the only injury, if you want call *that* an injury. Anyway, Marissa and I have some homework to do, so we'd better get going. See ya later!"

"Hold on, young ladies!" cried Mom. "Tell me more about the accident. Exactly what happened? Where were you sitting? Are you sure that neither of you were hurt? You would think that with all the tax money we pay that goes toward the Forrester school's budget, they would at least have decent tables for you poor kids. And that lovely Tiffany—I'll bet she was devastated. Maybe I'll call Mrs. Cooper, to check if her daughter is okay," she rambled on.

"Uh…no, Mom, you don't have to do that. Really, she's fine. She was smiling when she left the lunchroom. When I saw her in home room at the end of the day, she was even laughing about the whole ordeal. Right, Marissa?"

"Sure, yeah. Okay, let's get to our project, Jodi. I have to be home early today. My parents are taking me out to an expensive restaurant for dinner," said Marissa, rushing to get started with our afternoon investigation.

"Mommy, come here now! You have to help me study for my stupid vocabulary test. I need to use the word 'deceive' in a sentence!" screamed Seth from his room. "How about 'Joey and Bobby were deceived when their mother took them to the dentist instead of driving them to the bowling alley. How does that sound?" he asked, prompting Mom to run upstairs in his direction.

"I don't think so, Seth. Just give me a second, I'll be right up," she said, exasperated.

Marissa and I grabbed hands, tripping over each other's feet as we escaped from any more of my mother's probing questions. We really do have a project to work on, but not one that involved anything remotely connected to math, science, or English. It was time to chart my romantic destiny. Was Jason a part of it? Or was he just a wrong turn, and had I already wasted too much time and trouble? Something was amiss in the universe. Jason was acting weirder and weirder by the second. What was happening to my good old friend? It seemed the attraction that I thought he had for me was being rapidly replaced by his new interest in Tiffany. This was definitely a job for Madame Shumsky.

I sat down at my desk, pushed aside the mind-numbing science assignment on the family tree that would have to wait for a later time, and booted up my trusty computer. Marissa and I logged onto Madame Shumsky's Love and Compatibility website, scrolled down to Libra and Scorpio, and got ready to learn what the stars held for our romantic future. But first, I decided to check out what the psychic had written for today's SCORPIO HOROSCOPE on the site.

You have never been more ready for a complete change in your life. Gone is the cautious you. Beware! Situations that have confused you recently will finally become crystal clear.

"Thank goodness. I need things to become crystal clear instead of foggy. I think we are finally going to get some answers today. I feel more hopeful now."

I continued to read aloud from Shumsky's web page. "'When Libra and Scorpio come together in a love affair, they tend to make a very emotionally connected and mutually satisfying union. Union? What is she talking about? Connected? This is beginning to get too complicated."

"Keep going, Jodes. Are you sure that you have the right sign on that page? Maybe Madame Shumsky can get right to the heart—get it?—of your problem," said Marissa. "Erin, Amber, and I are starting to worry that you are placing too much importance on astrological forecasts. Why don't you just look at Jason's immature, attention-getting actions? As my mother would say, actions speak louder than words."

"I am going to ignore what you just said, Marissa, and keep reading. 'Though Scorpio is a brooder who can get lost in the confusion of her own emotions... Hey, I may be a little moody, but I'm not that bad," I said, before completing the reading. "Libra's tendency for balance and harmony helps keep Scorpio even. Scorpio can return the favor to Libra with her characteristic power of focus, a trait Libra usually lacks. This is not making any sense. Here, Marissa, you read."

Marissa rolled the desk chair in front of the monitor and focused on the web page. With enthusiasm, she continued to read: "Libra is happiest when in a well-balanced relationship."

"I can be well balanced and harmonious. Sorry to interrupt; continue, please."

"Scorpios thrives on emotional and physical intimacy with their mates."

"Hold it right there. I am so not ready for this part of my horoscope. I just want to be asked to dance, have Jason call me his girlfriend and be extra-nice to me around the lockers! Physical intimacy? Please, give me a break!"

"Jodi, I'm not done reading, just pipe down for a minute." Marissa continued, "These two are very compatible. They can make a very loyal, close, and satisfying partnership. Uh, Jodi, I don't think Jason is being particularly loyal by hanging on to Tiffany at her party or asking her to dance at his bar mitzvah," said Marissa.

"Yeah, thanks for pointing that out to me. Like, it's not starting to hit me over the head."

"This is not a boring relationship," read Marissa.

"I'll say it isn't boring. Throwing up on my shoes and jumping through flaming hoops were my first two clues as to how interesting life with Jason could be."

"Wait, there's still more," Marissa declared. "Libra is up-front and open."

"Open? Please! Maybe he's open to Tiffany these days, but I feel shut out. What kind of destiny is this?"

"Don't be jealous of that little witch, Jodi. You're ten times better than that phony," Marissa assured me. "Scorpio is intense and secretive."

"Wait one second. I am not secretive. Jason knows how I feel about him. We've been friends forever. What in heavens is happening?" I was getting more and more worked up as I studied the words that I imagined spilling directly out of Madame Shumsky's mouth.

"Sometimes they have trouble understanding one another, so they may need to pay close attention to their communication," continued Marissa.

"That's it! There's my answer. We have a lack of communication. I have to try harder to let him know that we are meant to be together. Oh good, now we are getter somewhere."

"Jodi, don't get your hopes up. I still think that you are wasting your time with that loser. He really isn't worth all the trouble that you are putting yourself through. Maybe Madame Shumsky's turban is too tight for her empty head. This lovey-dovey stuff is starting to ruin my appetite. And if my parents are taking me out to Chez Louise tonight, I want to be really, really hungry. Gotta run, talk to ya later."

"Can't you stay and help me think up the right questions to send in to Madame Shumsky? I can ask three questions per session at no extra charge. They guarantee that she will write back."

"I really wish I could, but I promised my parents I wouldn't be late. Sorry," Marissa said, as she quickly gathered her things and left my room.

I sat alone, staring at the computer monitor. Nothing is making any sense. I wonder if there was a mistake made on my original birth chart. If anyone can unravel this mystery for me, it's Madame Shumsky. I began typing on the keyboard.

Dear Madame Shumsky,

My name is Jodi Milner and my birthday is November 18, 1995. I am a Scorpio but of course you know that. I am so confused right now because my romantic destiny points to Libra as my soul mate. The problem is that the boy of my dreams does not even look in my direction anymore. In fact, he has been acting like the biggest jerk in the world. I've never admitted this before, not even to my very best friends. But honestly, I don't think that I even like him anymore.

Question 1: Am I doing anything wrong?

Question 2: Should I find another Libra to like?

Question 3: Am I spending too much time worrying about this?

Thank you,

Your faithful zodiac believer,

Jodi

I stared at what I had written and was tempted to hit the delete button, but then without any more thought, I hit the enter key with determination. After shutting down the computer, I flopped onto my bed. Hugging my favorite pillow, I closed my eyes. *Maybe a dream will hold the answers to my destiny.*

* * *

CHAPTER 12
DINNER AT CHEZ LOUIS

 Today's Horoscope:

Scorpio (October 24 – November 22) No matter what
thrills you've seen on television, read in suspense novels, or
experienced in life, they're no match for what lies ahead
today. Don't question the decisions of those
who love you.

"Wow, this restaurant is even fancier than I expected
it to be. Dad, I am so glad one of your clients gave
you a gift certificate to this place," gushed Marissa, as she
looked around the blue and yellow dining room.

"I feel like we're in a charming French country inn," said
Mrs. Torlucci.

"I'm glad my two special girls both like it here. The sky's the
limit, order anything you want from the menu," Mr. Torlucci
said, glancing nervously at his wife.

After scarfing down a delicious Caesar salad, a tender fi-
let mignon, and the largest baked potato she had ever seen,
Marissa's mouth was still watering for the chocolate soufflé she
had ordered at the beginning of the meal.

The proper French waiter set her dessert before her with a
grand flourish. She pierced the outside layer of the soufflé with
her spoon and warm chocolate oozed out over the rim of the

dish. The smell was intoxicating. Lost in the moment, she was suddenly interrupted by her all-too-serious-sounding dad.

"Marissa, Mom and I have something to discuss with you. It's about your Family Tree science project," said Mr. Torlucci.

"I know we have been avoiding you when you've been asking about your ancestors. Well, there is a good reason for that," said Marissa's mother. "Please sit back and listen to what we have to tell you. Marissa, honey, the day you were born was the happiest day of our lives," she said emotionally. "But I wasn't the one who carried you for nine months. Someone else did."

"What are you talking about?" cried a shocked Marissa.

"Sweetheart, just let Mom continue with our story," begged Mr. Torlucci.

"You see, I tried to have a baby for five years, but was not successful. Nothing happened. We wanted to have a child more than anything else in this world. When I couldn't get pregnant, the doctors suggested that we try adoption," explained Mrs. Torlucci.

Sitting at the table at Chez Louis, Marissa listened to her parents surprising tale as if she were in a horror movie. Her mouth opened wide, and it began to drop down lower and lower. The waiters seemed to be moving in slow-motion and the background noise, which had been quite loud, now seemed muffled.

As her parents concluded their explanation, Marissa sat frozen in her seat. Feelings and words were welling up inside her, but she couldn't seem to get them out. After a long, uncomfortable silence, Marissa found her voice. She was furious.

"Wait a minute! You're telling me that I'm adopted? I can't believe what I'm hearing!" Marissa yelled. She stood up and pushed back her chair, which made a loud thud that echoed throughout the dining room as it crashed to the floor.

The diners at the surrounding tables turned to watch, as an angry Marissa demanded of her parents, "How could you? You've lied to me my whole life! I just can't believe this!"

"Marissa, everyone in the restaurant is starting to stare. I am so sorry that we decided to tell you here, because we are creating a scene. Let me pay the bill and we will all go to the car and continue this conversation," said a very upset Mr. Torlucci.

He reached for his wallet to pay the bill, and then guided his distraught wife and enraged daughter toward the exit. Marissa's mother tried to put her arm around her daughter, but it was shoved away as the crying girl ran out of the dining room.

Angrily, Mrs. Torlucci turned to her husband and said, "I told you we should have broken the news to Marissa about the adoption in the school psychologist's office, instead of this fancy public place. And I told you that we shouldn't have waited this long to tell her the truth. She's almost thirteen years old and deserved to know our secret long ago."

* * *

The Torluccis had been prepared to tell Marissa that she was adopted as soon as she could understand what the word "adoption" meant. This was the recommendation of the adoption agency. As time went on, however, Mr. Torlucci never seemed to think it was the right moment.

Now, with Marissa at the age of twelve, they were faced with the hard task of finally informing her that they were not her birth parents. The family tree science project had forced them to divulge the truth.

As Marissa started researching her heritage she was asking lots of questions about her hair color, facial features, and personality when she rummaged through old family pictures. Up until now, the Torluccis had both become excellent storytellers, and at times had forgotten their detailed explanations of the whys and wherefores of Marissa's looks and characteristics. Curiously, even though the young girl had dark hair and an olive complexion, she really didn't have the high cheekbones or longish noses that most of the Torlucci or the Biro (her mother's maiden name) clans possessed.

* * *

Outside the restaurant, they found Marissa sitting on the curb in front of the valet station. "Give me some money. I have to get out of here. I'm taking a taxi to Jodi's house. One thing I can trust is that Jodi is my best friend. She would never lie to me. That I know for sure!"

"Marissa, we will be happy to drop you at Jodi's, if you think that will make you feel better. But, just know that your father and I love you and we need to continue this discussion later. Call us when you want to be picked up from Jodi's. It doesn't matter what time it is," said Mrs. Torlucci, holding back her tears.

Arriving at the Milner home, Marissa could already smell the luscious aromas of the burning candles coming from Jodi's room. The choice of fragrance was always a clue to Jodi's mood. Jasmine meant she was feeling calm, lavender meant that she needed to unwind or de-stress, vanilla was invigorating, and eucalyptus was a sign of peacefulness.

Some days, there was an entirely unfamiliar scent. Marissa always knew that these were "up" days for Jodi, because she'd always try a new smell when she was feeling happy and optimistic about life. There were other scents that were warning signs; licorice was always a high alert, and gardenia always meant "go home and call me later!" The scent today was jasmine.

When I saw Marissa, I immediately sensed that I had chosen the wrong candle for the mood that my best friend appeared to be in. Something was wrong, very wrong. Marissa was in tears. I thought someone in the Torlucci family had died.

"Sit down, Marissa. What happened? I am very worried about you. Did someone die?"

Marissa plopped down on the bed and squeezed the pillow so tightly that it looked like the feathers would start flying out from all the pressure.

"I feel like I'VE died, not someone else!" cried Marissa.

"What are you talking about?" I asked.

"I don't know who I am. I don't know who I am." Marissa said, in a voice that sounded like she was a walking zombie. "Jodi, I'm adopted," she blurted out.

I sat quietly, waiting for more information about this crazy news. I was stunned and confused as Marissa revealed the whole story of what she had just learned about herself.

"And can you believe they told me at Chez Louis? I would choke before I would ever set foot in that restaurant again. I used to think it was so elegant and delicious...," Marissa sobbed, and couldn't finish her sentence. "Of all things, the science project about our family tree forced my so-called parents to come clean! Unbelievable!"

After our tears had dried, Marissa felt relieved and surprised at how easy it was to share her newfound secret with me.

"I feel for you, Marissa. In fact, I'm very angry at your parents, too."

"I can't talk about this anymore tonight. I am so tired. I want to go home. Could you please call my parents and tell them to pick me up now?" asked Marissa.

As soon as the front door closed behind Marissa, I ran into the kitchen, where my mother was putting the final touches on her frank and bean casserole for tomorrow night's dinner. Mom had a substitute teaching job the next morning, and always liked to prepare a meal in advance when she was working.

"Mom, can you believe that Marissa was adopted? I'm in shock! Why would they lie to her all these years? Why? Did you know anything about this?"

"Jodi, my dear Jodi, no. Believe me, I had no idea whatsoever about Marissa's adoption. The only way that I can think of explaining why the Torluccis did this is that, on certain occasions, family or friends hide important truths from us. They may think that sometimes the truth will hurt. Holding back the whole story might shield their loved ones from unnecessary pain," my mother explained.

When my mom opened her mouth to speak her face looked like she was on fire. She reminded me of a cartoon character whose head might explode.

"I would rather know everything! How can you say that lying to your own kid about something so serious could be a good thing? You've got to be kidding! I'm going to my room!" I stormed out of the kitchen and up to my room, slamming my bedroom door behind me.

The loud noise reverberated through Sharon's spine, sending what felt like an electrical shock wave through her body. She immediately dialed the private phone number to her husband's dental office, where he had gone to deal with an emergency root canal.

* * *

CHAPTER 13
THE FAKE BIRTHDAY

 Today's Horoscope:

Scorpio (October 24–November 22) Disruptions and a lack
of peace can follow you home. Be careful, you may be putting
your trust into the wrong hands. Be prepared with a Plan B.
You'll need it!

"Barry, we have to talk! We have a problem!" Sharon
shouted into the phone.

"I'm in the middle of Mrs. Jarvis' root canal. It will have to
wait until after tomorrow," he said.

"No, we have to talk now. Mrs. Jarvis can wait, Barry, she
will have to."

"Sharon, calm down. You sound hysterical," he said.

"I am hysterical," she responded.

"Has there been an accident?"

"No!" yelled Sharon, losing her patience.

"Well, that's good news. We'll talk later, honey. I'll be home
at ten thirty." The line went dead before Sharon could get in
another word.

* * *

Sharon slumped like a Raggedy Ann doll to the floor, lean-
ing against the kitchen cabinet, and started to think back to the

beginning of their deception. How did we let this seemingly innocent plan get so out of hand? It had seemed like such a good idea at the time.

When Becky was a year old, Sharon took her to "Mommy and Me" classes at the local Jewish community center. As they sat on the floor in a circle, bouncing their burping babies to the tune of "the wheels on the bus go round and round," the mothers often talked about their older children. Sharon learned that the cutoff date to start kindergarten was December 31. The other mothers said that it would be a good idea to push Becky ahead one grade in school, because her birth date of January 10th missed the deadline by less than three weeks. She didn't take their advice seriously when Becky was ready to start school. Sharon had discussed the idea with her husband, Barry, and they thought it was nonsense at the time, even though their daughter seemed advanced for her age.

"What's the rush about starting school so early?" Barry had asked. "She'll have plenty of years in school. Just let her be a baby for another year."

The Milners realized that they had made a big mistake shortly after their little girl was enrolled in school. They decided after the fact that they probably should have started Becky in school a year earlier. Becky was very mature for her age and tended to play with older children. Even her nursery school teachers commented more than once how Becky should have skipped a grade. On Becky's birthday, Sharon brought chocolate-covered donuts for a class party at the Tinkerbelle Preschool. When she entered the classroom, she saw the children surrounding their teacher, Miss Caren. The kids were covered with finger paint and laughing out loud. They were climbing all over her and trying to draw a green mustache on her face. Becky, however, was sitting quietly in the far corner, with her face buried in a book, *The Runaway Bunny*. She lifted her eyes above the book for a split second and glanced at the others with a look that clearly meant, "What a bunch of babies."

Two years later, when Sharon was pregnant with Jodi, the Milners realized two things. One, Sharon would be delivering their new baby in early January once again. Two, they would take the advice of the "Mommy and Me" mothers this time. If their second child was anything like Becky, it would be better to have her or him start school early. But how could they get around the cutoff date?

One day, when Barry was working on one of his longtime patients in his dental office, he was thinking aloud about the school cutoff policy. As luck would have it, Ned Biggins was sitting in the dental chair, with his mouth wide open. The patient worked in the county clerk's office and had access to birth and death certificates as part of his job.

Mr. Biggins wiped the spittle off the side of his mouth before saying, "I can hack into a website that will print out an authentic birth certificate. Those unsuspecting employees down at the school administration building will never discover a thing. Your kid is good to go," offered the man. "Just give me the heads up when your baby is born."

Barry thought about what Biggins was offering for a few moments as he completed the dental examination. "Ned, what are you suggesting?"

"Doc, it's the least I can do for my favorite dentist. Believe me, it's done all the time. No problemo," smiled Mr. Biggins, as he put his old baseball cap back on his head and left the office.

A few months later, on January 8, Sharon went to the hospital to deliver her baby. Barry reluctantly called Mr. Biggins and told him to set the wheels in motion for the switcheroo. Sure enough, eight weeks after Jodi was born they received her "official" birth certificate in the mail. The date of November 18, 1995, was written on the document. It was just as Ned Biggins had promised.

Who knew that their sweet baby girl would transform into an astrology-crazed preteen, whose world revolved around the signs of the zodiac? The fifty-one days between when Jodi was actually born and her fake birthday made her a counterfeit Scorpio instead of a true Capricorn. This was a humongous difference for such a horoscope maniac. Twelve years later, their honest efforts (or dishonest efforts, rather) had come back to haunt them.

Sharon picked herself up from the floor and glanced at the clock on the wall. "Oh, no. I can't believe how late it is!" The frank and bean casserole that she was preparing ahead of time, and the surprise that they had in store for Jodi, were sure to give the whole family a double portion of gas and grief.

When the whole family came home from work and school the next day, Sharon had finished rehearsing what to divulge and how to tell the story about the fake birthday to Jodi.

During dinner there was very little conversation. The air felt heavy and strained. When Seth spilled his soda all over the table, flooding the French fries and leaving Sharon's lap soaked, she bolted up and screamed, "Can't you be careful, Seth? Pay attention for once! Somebody get some paper towels! Why are you all sitting there, staring like zombies? Can't you people do anything?"

Becky obediently ran to get the paper towels and started mopping up the mess. Barry could tell that his wife's horrid mood must have something to do with her emergency phone call the night before. The root canal that he had been working on the night before was much more complicated and took longer than he had anticipated. The dentist arrived home after everyone was fast asleep, and this was the first opportunity he had to discover what was bothering Sharon.

By the time the table was wiped dry and everyone was seated to finish supper, I decided that I had lost my appetite. My horoscope was *right-on* this morning. There seems to be a disruption in this kitchen, so I wanted to go upstairs and check if Madame Shumsky had answered my website questions. Maybe she had written a Plan B for me.

"I'm not hungry, may I be excused?"

"Yes, sweetie," answered Barry. "Go do your homework, and make sure that Seth has something to keep him busy. Mom and I have to go into our bedroom to discuss something that's private. Becky, please help clean up the dishes."

I gave my sister a worried look. Seth, oblivious to what was going on, had already dashed up the stairs to turn on the TV in his room.

A private conversation, I thought. *Is Mom going to tell him about Marissa? Why is she so hyper? And what's with Dad's mysteriousness? This week is getting stranger and stranger every day!*

* * *

Barry took Sharon by the hand and they disappeared behind their bedroom door.

"That's it! We have to tell her," Sharon announced.

"What are you talking about, Sharon? I have no clue," he said, in his usual laid-back manner.

Sharon filled Barry in on Marissa's earlier confession, and how hard a time Jodi was having accepting the news of the adoption. She explained that their daughter was not simply upset that her best friend was an adopted child. What had made Jodi so angry was the fact that Marissa's parents had deceived her for so long.

"Jodi will get over it, Sharon. What has any of this got to do with us? I am still very confused!" said Barry.

"Are you on another planet? It has everything to do with us! We've been lying to our own daughter since she was born. We changed her birthday, if you remember. Or have you forgotten?" hissed Sharon.

"Of course I haven't forgotten. Just settle down," Barry said, as he placed a calming hand on Sharon's shoulder.

Pushing his hand away, she hollered, "We are guilty! How could we have kept this secret from our daughter for so many years? It's about time that we told her the truth! Her bat mitzvah is around the corner, and she doesn't even know that she's celebrating her real birthday on the wrong day!"

"Sharon, you are overreacting. It's not that big of a deal. It's only a fake birthday."

"No big deal! Do you know your daughter at all? First of all, we've lied. Second of all, she is so into this astrology foo-foo. She makes all her decisions based on her daily chart!"

"Yeah, so? I'm trying to see where we've been criminals here. We did it so she could start school early and not be bored. We did it for her own good!" said Barry, defending their actions.

"Barry, she's a Capricorn, just like Becky. She's not a Scorpio!"

"Capricorn, Scorpio—it's all Mickey Mouse nonsense. Get a hold of yourself; you are being a bit too melodramatic."

"I am not overreacting. This is very serious, and she believes in this New Age thinking. Jodi spends most of her allowance on astrology books, smelly incense, and colored crystals." Sharon was beginning to lose it again.

"Okay, okay. I see your point, but still, it's not that big of a deal. We'll just tell her that her birthday is the eighth of January. Maybe, to make things up to her, we can throw her two parties this year."

Sharon sat silently, thinking to herself that he did not realize the gravity of this for Jodi. She would be devastated. With that, she stood up and announced, "I'm calling the rabbi and setting up an appointment with her as our counselor. We are telling Jodi this week. I've made up my mind."

* * *

CHAPTER 14
E X P O S U R E

Today's Horoscope:

Capricorn (December 22–January 19) Before you point fingers at who might be to blame for the unexpected change in your plans, take a few moments to reflect on how this turn of events might be a blessing in disguise.

At three p.m. the next day, I walked out the door of Forrester Middle School and searched among the waiting cars for my mother's white Toyota RAV4. We were going to go to Temple Beth Or to meet with Rabbi Sari Benjamin. Supposedly, we would be discussing how my bat mitzvah community service project was progressing. Little did I know the real reason for our meeting.

Mom and I were led into Rabbi Benjamin's office, where we were scheduled to talk about my tzedakah project. Tzedakah means doing good deeds. Many Jewish boys and girls not only complete their rite of passage by reading from the Torah (Holy Jewish Scrolls), they also do good deeds for others. I intended to give something back to the community by working for *Hands Helping Homeless* (HHH) in the nearby town of Groden.

I have so much to be grateful for that I want to help others in any way that I can. I had told this to Rabbi Benjamin at a previous meeting, and she agreed that *Hands Helping Homeless* would be the ideal opportunity to fulfill my goal.

Today's meeting was designed to discuss the specifics of my community service. How many hours a week would I work on helping to build a house for the homeless? How would I go about getting other friends to help? Wouldn't it be great if I could meet the new homeowners when the house was finished? I love watching that television show *Extreme Makeover*, where they redo a needy family's house. It gives me such a great feeling when they move the big bus and the family sees their new home for the first time. That's what tzedakah is all about. At least, that's what I thought was the purpose of the meeting.

* * *

Actually, Sharon had called the rabbi for suggestions on how to tell her daughter that she had a fake birthday. The Milners had to finally come clean about their elaborate scam.

Originally, Jodi had been unable to understand why her bat mitzvah date was in January instead of November, nearer to her birthday. Sharon had said that the synagogue secretary assigned January 22 as the first available date. At the time, Jodi didn't question this explanation.

When Sharon called the rabbi to confess the birthday switch, Rabbi Benjamin was surprised, but seemed to understand the Milners reasoning. She agreed that telling Jodi about her fake birthday was appropriate, and the sooner the better.

* * *

"Honesty is the best policy," said Rabbi Benjamin. "Jodi will be angry and confused at first, but in time she'll realize that what you two orchestrated was with her best interest in mind." So that is exactly what Sharon did.

* * *

I entered the study and sat down next to my mother. For some reason there was an uneasy feeling in the room. The rabbi seemed too serious or something, and so did Mom. Without any small talk, Rabbi Benjamin began.

"Jodi, my dear, your mother has something she needs to tell you. I'm here just as your religious counselor. I can answer any questions you might have after she's finished."

Mom, bursting at the seams, began talking, almost cutting off the rabbi in mid-sentence.

"Jodi, I have to tell you something. You are a bit younger than you think. Your birthday is not November eighteenth, it is January eighth." Mom continued, explaining the saga of the change in my birthday. The how, the why, and the when. She gave me all the complicated details of the scheme.

Ten minutes later, I sat in the rabbi's study as limp as my old Raggedy Ann doll that was hidden on the shelf in the back of my closet. I didn't know what to say. Even if I could have formed the words, I was in no mood to speak to my mother right now.

Okay, this isn't as terrible as what happened to Marissa, I thought. But what is wrong with these people? Are all parents liars?

In the car on the way home, I sat speechless while my mother rambled on nervously.

"Jodi, darling, we are so sorry. We didn't realize that you would take this so hard. We love you and only want everything to work out for you. Please say something," she pleaded. "If you think about it for a minute, it's really kind of funny." She let out a high-pitched snort.

I was not amused, and turned my head to look out the window, giving my mother the cold shoulder and the silent treatment.

As the car pulled into the long driveway at 11 Walnut Lane, I felt like a caged animal. I couldn't get out of the SUV fast enough. I opened the door, stormed out, and ran through the house to my room. Of course, I threw in some door slamming for effect before launching myself onto my bed.

Picking up the phone, I called the one person in the world that I knew would understand my anger.

"Marissa, hi. You are not going to believe what I have to tell you."

"Okay, shoot. What is it?" Marissa asked.

"I can't tell you on the phone, it is too…it is too…" I stopped, because I felt my throat begin to close and my eyes overflowing with tears. I had been holding off crying since we left the rabbi's study.

"Jodi, are you still there? Where'd you go?" asked Marissa, sounding alarmed.

"Yeah, I'm here, but just come over right away. Please. Tell your mom that I need help with a report that's due tomorrow." I was begging now. "Please, I really need you."

"But…uh…Jodi, I don't think I can come now. You see, my mom made us an appointment to have a manicure date."

"A what? You're kidding, right?" I was becoming increasingly annoyed by the second.

"Well, Jodi, it's like ever since she confessed about my being adopted, she has this need to spend more special, or, you know, what they call it quality time with me," responded Marissa apologetically.

"You're serious? A manicure date is supposed to make you feel better about finding out that you're adopted! That is so totally lame!"

"Jodi, calm down. Whatever is bothering you obviously can't wait until tomorrow. Mom will have to reschedule our together time for another day. I'll ride my bike over right now and bring the notes for my science project with me. Believe me, she's giving me lots of leeway ever since she confessed the truth about my ancestry. I have to redo the whole tree now, since my parents aren't even my parents," Marissa said, and she hung up.

Still holding the receiver, I sat in silence for several minutes. I then pulled out some of my star charts and astrological planners, and lit a few licorice-scented candles. I logged on to my computer and pulled up my favorite website that predicted my week ahead. *I've got to find out who I am. I have to figure all this out.*

With the strong aroma filling the air, I stopped to turn on some of my favorite music. Slowly, I scattered all the important books and papers in front of me and prepared to delve into the world of this stranger who had been born on January 8.

Maybe Madame Shumsky had answered my questions by now. Could it be that the reason it had taken her so long to get back to me was that she knew that my astrological sign was out of whack? This explains so much. Oh, great; look, there are three new messages waiting for me in my e-mail inbox! There she is. Madame Shumsky lives.

"I'm here!" yelled Marissa from downstairs.

I was so focused on the computer monitor that I didn't hear the doorbell ring. "C'mon up. Look what Madame Shumsky finally wrote to me. Put your backpack down and pull up a chair."

Peering at the screen, we read the e-mails together.

> *"Dear Jodi,*
> *There is major disruption in your universe. You write that your birth date is November 18, yet when I began to chart your romantic destiny, I kept getting an "error" message.*

"An error message?" asked Marissa. "What is she, a computer programmer or a psychic?"

"Quiet, Marissa. I am trying to concentrate."

> *Jodi, please ask your parents to provide you with your original birth certificate. Please check the date and time of your birth, as well as the year. Resubmit with the new information. E-mail #2: Error. E-mail #3: Error. Resubmit.*

* * *

CHAPTER 15
NEW BEGINNINGS

 Today's Horoscope:

Capricorn (December 22–January 19) Clouds will lift swiftly.
Your self-confidence may feel shattered by situations over
which you have no control. But don't worry little goat, you
will find happiness when the sun rises.

"Jodi, its Mom. Can I come in, please?"
"No!"
"Jodi, I'd like you to open the door."
"No, go away."
"Jodi, give me a break."

* * *

Only two days had passed since I learned about my real
birthday. I was still so angry at my parents that I couldn't even
eat at the dinner table with them. They were feeling so guilty
about their deception that they let me grab my meal and bring
it up to my bedroom. Taking food out of the kitchen was definitely a no-no in the Milner household, but this was a special
case. I won't be able to get away with this arrangement for too
long, because Mom freaks if she thinks that bugs might get
into the house.

"I don't know what more you want from me. You can't live and eat alone in your room forever. Your father, brother, and sister all miss you and want you to come downstairs and join them. At least have dessert with us. I made your favorite, the chocolate killer cake."

Mom was desperately trying to re-open the lines of communication.

"No, thank you. I'm not interested. I don't care to eat dessert with liars. Please leave me alone. I have a lot of thinking to do about the mess I'm in." I heard my mom stomp back down the stairs.

"This isn't going as well as we predicted, Barry. Jodi is a mess. She's really starting to unravel," said Sharon.

Barry said, "Honey, you're overreacting again. Of course she's upset; she just found out that we lied to her. What did you expect her to do? Thank us? Now, just give her some time and space to cool off."

"Barry, *what have we done*? How could we have lied to her about something so sacred?"

"Mom, this chocolate cake is the best. Can I have another piece?" asked Seth.

"Me, too," said Becky. "The smell of the warm chocolate is so delicious that it almost covers up whatever candle Jodi is burning up there. The waxy odor is starting to creep through the ceiling."

"This smell is making me nauseous, too. Couldn't she be angry with a smell like lemon instead?" Sharon wondered aloud, holding back the beginnings of a gag.

Upstairs in my room, I was charting my new sign. It felt like I had entered some sort of time warp. Who was this stranger born on January 8? Could I be this person? How could it be possible? *How in the world could I be a Capricorn?*

Suddenly, I felt a sharp pain pierce my stomach like a knife.

"OH, NO! NO! NO! I am the same sign as Becky!" I heard my voice escalating to such a pitch that it blared through the house like a siren. This wail was because I suddenly realized that Becky and I were what the astrology sites referred to as "same sign sisters." *The same sign...how could that be? We are as different as night and day. It just can't be, it can't be. Maybe Mom and Dad changed Becky's birth date, too, and haven't told her yet? Nothing would surprise me lately.*

Stomp! Stomp! Stomp! Rats! Mom must have heard me. I can hear her charging up the steps now.

Bang! Bang! Bang!

"Open this door," Mom shrieked. .

"Jodi, you will open this door now. I mean it, or I'll call the fire department and they'll break it down with axes."

I opened the door slowly, catching a quick peek at Mom. She was really upset, and I felt bad that I had made her look that way. But I couldn't let myself feel sorry for her now; I had too much to figure out. My body felt tingly and my legs were starting to go numb. If I didn't lie down now, I might faint. I grabbed my favorite stuffed scorpion and fell onto my pillows. What am I doing? I don't want this fake scorpion. I am not even a Scorpio, I am a Capricorn. With all these stuffed animals around me, I should at least have a goat! I am such a mess.

"Watch it, Jodi!" Mom cried, as the flying scorpion barely missed her head. I had thrown it across the room and didn't realize it was heading in her direction. "I can be patient so long, but now you are skating on thin ice."

Mom was still trying to figure out what had provoked my scream and was a little dazed from the flying scorpion attack. Looking around the room, she saw all the astrological paraphernalia and noted the computer screen was on a site that advertised: "Know yourself, read your daily horoscope now!" And, of course, the sign highlighted was CAPRICORN. Two dates, January 8 and January 10—both my real birthday and Becky's—were boldly highlighted.

"Okay, Jodi, I get it," said Mom, as she joined me on the bed and placed an arm around me in a gentle hug. "I love you, Jodi. Dad and I never meant to hurt you."

I started to sniffle. And Mom got into the act, too.

"Don't cry, Mom. I'm just so confused. I'm angry with you and Dad. I'm just feeling all mixed up right now. I mean, if I'm a Capricorn and Becky is a Capricorn, then how can we be so different—or are we? Birth dates just two days apart, not two months? Are you sure I was born in January? Mom, maybe you've forgotten when I was born, since it was so long ago. Can't you just get my original birth certificate? It will have the correct date."

"Perhaps we should have just left well enough alone," Mom muttered.

"Are you okay, Mom? You look very flushed. You're not getting sick, are you?"

"I'm fine. It's probably just a hot flash. I'm just disturbed that you are so miserable. I'm so sorry, Jodi."

"I'm feeling very lost right now, Mom. This is going to take time. Does Becky know my true birth date? Has she been keeping this secret, too?"

"I'm actually not sure. We've always celebrated your birthday in November. I don't think she paid much attention. When you were born she was only a toddler. Anyway, what can I do to make it up to you? I'll do anything to make you happy," said my anguished mother.

I stopped suffering long enough to think about what I wanted. What I really wanted was for this mess not to have happened in the first place. But hey, it was far too late for that. One thing that I had been wanting for so long my mother had strictly forbidden.

"Okay, Mom, I know what I want and I've wanted it for a long time!"

"Yes?" she asked, looking fearful of what she had promised.

"I want a belly-button ring. You said you would do anything to make me happy, after what you and Dad did to me. Well, a belly-button ring would help make me a little happier." I felt the beginning of a tiny grin on my face. It had been days since I had wanted to smile about anything. "But don't think that I am letting you off the hook so easily. Having a fake birthday is absolutely blowing me away."

Mom swallowed hard, with one hand pounded her chest and clutched a clump of her hair with the other hand. She had forbidden this request before when Becky had asked her for the very same thing. Mom felt this fad was unsanitary and disgusting, but at this point I knew that she'd give in.

With that, she grabbed the car keys from her purse and resignedly said, "Jodi, let me call your dermatologist. I know he will at least be able to do this for you with sterile instruments.

An hour later we were at the mall picking out the cutest ever belly button ring and off we went to the doctor's office. I was actually starting to feel happy. Maybe being a Capricorn isn't all bad!

* * *

CHAPTER 16
FASHION STATEMENT

Today's Horoscope:

Capricorn (December 22–January 19) Mom's the word. You're quietly disciplined now, conservative and classic in style. Your dress code should deliver a clear message: you're a card-carrying primster, letting her bun down only in private.

Joining my BFF's at our usual lunch table, I showed up wearing an orange turtleneck sweater over brown tailored tweed pants and brown ballet flats. Gone were my usual jeans, cropped T-shirt, and sneakers. My wild curls were trapped in a severe-looking do, secured by a tortoiseshell hair clip. My friends were chattering on about the upcoming basketball game against our rival, Laurelton Middle School, when they noticed my odd-looking outfit.

"What are you wearing?" asked Erin. "Is this dress up like your mother day?"

"I checked my fashion horoscope last night, and this is what I am supposed to wear. I have it right here. Let me read it to you," I explained, and read it to them.

"What are you talking about? You look like a freak. Didn't you tell us last month that Scorpios were femme fatales and should dress in soft fabrics and look like free spirits? Your hair is pulled so tight that I think it is affecting your brain," said Amber.

"Capricorn horoscope!" yelled Erin, as she grabbed my notebook out of my hands and stared at the open page. "Now I am convinced you've checked out. Remember, Jodi, you are a Scorpio. We only hear about your sign and your predictions every day."

I was not fazed by the abuse I was taking from my friends, but could no longer hold my big secret inside. Slowly, I began to raise the hem of my sweater until my big surprise was revealed.

"Oh my God! You finally got a belly-button ring!" Erin, Amber, and Marissa shouted in unison.

"Have you lost your mind? Everyone knows you have to be eighteen years old to get a piercing. Did you get your parents' permission? How did you do it?" asked Amber. "I bet you got a fake ID."

I couldn't help but gloat. "That's what you think. Last night, my mom took me to the Piercing Palace Pagoda at the mall and we picked out this ring out together. Do you like it?" I asked, pointing to the tiny silver animal now attached to my body.

"Like it? I love it!" squealed Erin.

"Did it hurt?" asked Amber.

"I have to admit, it really, really hurt." I reached across the table and pinched Amber's arm firmly. "Much worse than that."

"Ouch! Stop it!" Amber screamed.

"It was a lot harder than having my ears pierced two years ago. I think it was totally worth it, though."

Staring at the little belly charm for a few moments, Erin cried out, "Jodi, it's a goat! Why would you pick a goat when your zodiac sign is a scorpion?"

"Boy, have I got a story to tell you guys," I said, sitting back comfortably in my chair. I looked at Marissa, silently signally her to let me disclose this bizarre tale without her letting on that she knew the whole story beforehand. It would take a long time to explain. We would all probably be late for the next period and would have to sit in detention with Vice Principal Sandalwood. I was sure that when they heard what I had to reveal about my fake birthday, they wouldn't mind a bit.

After I led my friends through my life-changing ordeal, they sat speechless. They looked like they were in shock.

"You're making this up, right?" said Marissa, pretending that she knew nothing, even though I had let her in on the whole story the other night. "Are we competing for the worst parents' award because mine just told me that I was adopted?"

"Don't be ridiculous. I couldn't have made up this story even if I tried. It still doesn't make any sense to me. I can't believe my parents would go to such extremes to get me into school a year early. Actually, Marissa, my parents finally told me the truth because I was so upset when I found out that your parents had lied to you for so long."

"So, let me get this straight. When is your real birthday?" asked Amber.

"It's January eighth, two weeks before my bat mitzvah. How sneaky were my parents? Even the rabbi was fooled. And can you believe that I am not a Scorpio, but a Capricorn? From now on, I have to think differently, act differently, and dress differently, too." I tightened the clip in my hair.

"Jodi, did you raid your mother's closet to find that pathetically gross outfit?" asked Tiffany, who had snuck up on us while we were deep in our discussion about my new discovery.

"Lay off, Tiffany. As long as you are dressed in your usual pink chic, don't worry about anyone else," said Erin.

The last person that I would want to know about my fake birthday is Miss Tiff. If she found out, the news would spread through the seventh grade like the measles did when we were in kindergarten.

"This is too much for us to swallow right now. Come on, everyone. We are already late for class," said Erin.

Tiffany persisted, saying, "Stop. You guys are definitely talking about some happening. I can feel the vibes in the air. I am not going to leave you alone until you let me in on it."

"Excuse me, girls," said Heath, as he passed by our table. "It looks like you are all in the middle of something intense, but I want to remind Jodi that we are supposed to meet up at three o'clock outside the school today. Don't be late! We have lots of work to do. I'm going to be late for math. Catch you later."

Amber turned to me with a puzzled expression and said, "Is he kidding? Did you sign up for something? What is going on here?"

"Don't tell me you have a date with Heath," said a snotty Tiffany.

"Well, that wouldn't be a bad thing. I think he's kind of cute," Amber said, standing up and getting ready to leave the cafeteria.

"Oh, now I remember. With everything going on, I almost forget about our tzedakah project, which is supposed to help others. Heath and I have been working with Hands Helping Homeless. We are building a beautiful new home for a poor family in Groden. It may be just the thing to take my mind off of my own problems." I had been so involved with my own drama that I had lost track of the real, serious issues that affect other people. I have been throwing temper tantrums from my cozy room in my great house. There are so many people who don't even have a place to sleep.

"Don't you mean Hands Helping Hopeless?" laughed Tiffany.

"I have to catch up with Heath, to tell him something else about HHH," I said. Heath always seems to be in the right place at the right time to save me from the trials of Tiffany. It is nice to know that I can depend on him, because Jason is missing in action.

"Don't leave yet. You still haven't told me what's going on. Don't leave me out of the loop. What problems?" asked Tiffany. But it was to an empty table, as the other girls had already left and I was on my way.

* * *

CHAPTER 17
HANDS HELPING HOMELESS

Walking toward the work site later that day, I was surprised to see how much progress had been made on the group of row homes that were being built by *Hands Helping Homeless* in this low-income neighborhood. The team leader, Joe Hanlon, was already issuing orders to the daily workers. There were twenty-two volunteers from various church and synagogue youth groups, all wearing old beat-up jeans and red T-shirts emblazoned with the HHH logo on the back. Hammers, nails, and screwdrivers were cleverly used to form the letter H on the shirts.

"Becky, I can't understand why you insisted on coming with me today. Why would you want to help me with my tzedakah project? I thought you had soccer practice on Thursdays. I'm still so upset over my fake birthday farce. I just wanted to come here today and get my hands dirty, while clearing my mind. I have to stop dwelling on what has been happening to me. I would like hammers and nails to replace thoughts of scorpions and goats."

"Come on, Jodes. I'm here to help. Get with the program," said Becky.

"Okay. Stick around. HHH can definitely use the extra help, but give me some space."

"Wait, Jodi. Don't take it out on me. It was Mom and Dad who betrayed you. I had nothing to do with it. Remember, I was only a little kid at the time," said Becky. "I took one look at you when you came home from the hospital and thought, what is this smelly pink bundle? I guess it was normal to really want a new little sister, but I was more interested in the new stuffed teddy bear that Mom and Dad gave me at the same time."

"I hear what you are saying. I felt the same way about Seth when Mom and Dad brought him home. And now, even though he is such a pain sometimes, I wouldn't send him back if I were given the choice. Speaking of wanting to do things over, I am sorry that I wasted so much time looking up the Scorpio horoscope each morning, so I could prepare myself for the day ahead. I wasn't even a Scorpio! I can't believe that I was such a jerk."

"Yeah, I always thought that was a big waste of time. You can't change the past. What's done is done, get over yourself! Now, just hand me the hammer and box of nails, and let's do something constructive," said my big sister.

I picked up the tools and proceeded to bang the nails on the floorboard as hard as I could hammer. It felt great to get my anger out. The more I thought about the previous few days, the harder I pounded and the better I felt.

I can't...*bang*...believe...*bang*...that they... *bang*...did this to me...*bang*!

"Oh, rats!" shouted Joe. "I dropped my wedding band all the way down the crawl space. Quick, someone get me a flashlight."

"Here's one, Joe," said Becky, who had jumped into action.

I looked up from my feverish hammering and joined the small group of volunteers who were now standing around Joe.

The team leader had placed his wedding band in his shirt pocket earlier. He was a newlywed and wasn't used to wearing a wedding band, or any ring for that matter. He had taken it off before starting work today.

"If my girl, Angie, finds out that my ring is missing, she'll blow a gasket," said Joe, starting to sweat even though it was a cool fall day.

"Let me get it," I said.

"No, Jodi. Thanks anyway. I can't allow you to go down there. Lots of loose rusted nails and broken-off pieces of wood have fallen through the cracks. For all I know, the basement might even be infested with rats," he warned.

"I want to help. I need to do this. Becky, support me on this."

"Joe, listen to me. My sister can do this. I know she will be able to get your precious ring. She's small and wiry. Jodi can weasel her way into the tiniest space," insisted Becky.

"Absolutely not. I don't think it would be safe," answered Joe.

Becky and I weren't listening to his warnings because we had already figured out a game plan. Becky found a long piece of rope and was busy tying it securely around my waist. The excitement and anticipation of doing something positive instead of dwelling on my problems had lifted my mood.

As Joe turned to continue his objections to our plan about what could go wrong with the ring-rescue mission, he saw me slithering down into the basement area. Joe quickly ran to Becky's side and grabbed hold of the rope when he realized we weren't listening to a word he had said.

When I whipped out the flashlight from my back jeans pocket, I laughed to myself. It's a good thing I decided not to go for the hip look by wearing my new designer jeans. I don't care if this old, torn, bleached-out pair gets ruined.

"Jodi, get up here this instant! I don't want to take a chance on you getting hurt!" yelled Joe, who was starting to be surrounded by the other teenaged volunteers.

"Have some faith in my sister. She'll find your precious ring, and save your you-know-what," assured Becky.

In the meantime, I was scurrying around below, with my flashlight shining on an assortment of old, smelly lunch remnants, broken floorboards, and rusty nails. Suddenly, a pair of dark red eyes was staring directly up at me from the ground. I froze, thinking that it was a filthy rat just waiting to jump at me and sink its sharp teeth into my wrist. I wanted to scream, but held it in for fear that the beast would attack me. All of a sudden, I heard a faint meow and the old cat scampered away. I guess the scary rat was only a lost cat that was probably more afraid of me. It had been sitting on Joe's prized gold wedding ring the whole time.

I was so relieved that I let out all the breath that I'd been holding inside. I wiped the sweat that was streaming down my face, and called up to the crowd that was waiting above.

"I found it! Quick, get me out of here!"

Heath ran over to Joe and Becky to help them tug on the rope. With their teamwork, I was able to carefully climb back up from the filthy basement. All the volunteers on our team cheered and hugged me, even though I was covered from head to toe in sawdust, dirt, and a few stray French fries—not a pretty sight.

"I knew you could do it, Jodes. I'm so proud of you!" exclaimed Becky.

I felt pretty proud of myself, too, as I handed the gold wedding ring to Joe. But more importantly, I was happy to be connecting with my sister for the first time in a very long time.

"Jodi, here comes the bus. Let me put our tools back in the work shed, and you go grab two seats on the bus. How about if we only talk about who should get kicked off *Dancing with the Stars*, who shouldn't get a rose on the *Bachelor*, and other silly stuff all the way home? Let's put fake birthdays behind us."

"Great idea, sis."

* * *

The scene at the Milner dinner table that night confused Sharon and Barry. They were glancing at Jodi from the corner of their eyes, expecting her to burst out in additional hysterics.

Instead, they saw Becky and Jodi kidding around about the incredible adventure that had taken place a few hours earlier. The couple felt like they weren't at 11 Walnut Lane, but on the set of a sitcom about the perfect family. Nobody even noticed that Seth was making pictures out of his peas and mashed potatoes, and then flattening them with his fork.

"Maybe the worst is over, and Jodi can get on with her life," Sharon said to her husband later that evening. "Now, I can start worrying about something else. There is a bat mitzvah to plan for."

* * *

CHAPTER 18
NOT A REAL DATE

 Today's Horoscope:

Capricorn (December 22–January 19) An on-again, off-again friendship or an affair of the heart will finally settle down when Venus moves in. But you may be ready to move on. It would be wiser to find someone who supports you rather than one who ignores you. And that person is out there.

My mother had promised to let me go shopping at the mall by myself after school today. That was something she never would have considered a month ago. Lately, she was giving me more and more responsibility. She was so happy that Becky and I were getting along so much better these days. I actually caught Mom checking her own horoscope at the breakfast table the other day. It probably read, "Don't be afraid. Let your daughter go to the mall by herself."

Even though she was reluctant at first, with each successful outing, Mom grew increasingly confident in my ability to stay out of trouble. She was much less worried about leaving me alone at the mall for a few hours. Usually, I would have shopped with at least one other girlfriend, but as it turned out, my BFF's were all going out of town for different family celebrations this weekend.

Great, I have three hours to kill at the mall. Let's see, first I need to find the absolute right top to go with my jeans for the school pep rally next week, then some new running shoes, and then I need some birthday cards.

Lost in my thoughts, I nearly smashed into Heath. He did not look the least bit upset by the near miss. In fact, one might think he intentionally got in my way.

"Hey, are you spaced out or something? You almost walked right into the fountain. Good thing I was here to save you. You might have drowned!"

"Please, Heath, you've been a superhero already once this week when you rescued me from Tiffany's claws in the school cafeteria. I'm beginning to think you're stalking me. Are you?"

"Superman or not, I'm not following you. I'm on my way to that new awesome movie, *The Slasher of Hidden Ridge*. My friends were supposed to meet me here, but they are missing in action. So typical of those guys. Why don't you come with me instead? You even told me you were dying to see it…remember?"

I just looked at him with a cautious glare. I didn't know what to say.

"Look, don't get weird, it's not like a real date. You're here, I'm here, and we both want to see this movie. Do you get it? I'll even buy the popcorn! This truly is a great offer. You're not going to turn down free popcorn, are you?" he said, with a hopeful smile. His little dimple was getting even more obvious by the second.

Hey, what's going on here? Heath is really cute. I had to think fast. *No one will know, my close friends are all out of town. No one even knows that I went to the mall, except for Mom, that is, and she wouldn't have to know either.*

"Jodi, are you coming with me or not? The show is starting in less than ten minutes. I'm going anyway, so what's it going to be?"

I looked at Heath. "You don't happen to have your cape handy, do you, Superman?"

Without hesitation, he replied, "I left my cape at home. But, never fear, for I have my super-warp-speed running shoes on. Give me your hand, Lois."

There was no time to think. I grabbed his hand and we set off at what felt like a supersonic pace, making it all the way across the mall in record time.

Fortunately, there were still seats left and time to spare for buying the popcorn Heath had promised. Just as he was paying for our snack, a bellowing scream was heard from clear across the expansive theater lobby.

"Jodieeeeeeeeeeeee!"

I immediately ducked down behind Heath. Oh no, anybody but her highness! It can't be. She's with Jason. That two-timing, double-crossing cretin. In history class, when I asked him what he was doing tonight, he said he had to study for his math test, and that he also had a science project due on Monday. The liar! He told me that he couldn't see the movie because he planned to be busy all weekend doing research on the Net. What a jerk!

Research, I'll show him research. I clenched my fists and bit down on my back teeth. I was ready to race across the lobby to deliver a wind-up clip to Jason's jaw.

Hold on. Wait just a minute. Let me rethink this. I keep forgetting that Jason is no longer my romantic destiny. Did I not read in today's horoscope about moving on? Well, no time like the present to do it. For all I care, he can have Tiffany. They make the perfect look-at-me couple.

In my old Scorpio way of thinking, Jason would have been the one for me. I tried to fit him into my daily horoscope. I should have known something was terribly off each day, when everything that had to do with Jason turned into a horror show. Now that I know my true sign is Capricorn, I am finally ready to move on. Yes, I am ready to do this!

Just then, Heath tapped me on the shoulder. "Come on Jodi, let's hurry in and find a seat." Heath apparently had ignored Tiffany and Jason, and was more interested in not missing the coming attractions.

* * *

"That movie was one of the best thrillers I have seen in a long time. I sat with my eyes glued to the big screen for the full one hundred and five minutes of the movie's running time. Did you like it as much as I did, Jodi?"

"Yeah, sure. It was terrific." I can't believe he hardly noticed that for most of the movie I was turning from side to side, trying desperately to locate the evil duo. I was testing myself to see how I would feel if I saw them sitting all cozy in the darkened theater. Needless to say, I could not concentrate on the movie, and I never did spot the lovebirds.

"Jodi, would you mind watching the credits? My family knows the guy that did the music editing of this film. I'd like to wait and see his name on the big screen. Okay?"

Still worried that Tiffany would be waiting outside the theater for us, I breathed a sigh of relief. They would be long gone by now.

"Of course, the credits! Yeah, I love watching credits. Yes, yes, every one of them...let's stay till they kick us out! I wouldn't even mind watching the whole movie again. It was so exciting." I sounded like a babbling idiot. Get a grip.

"No, I am too hungry. Let's go," said Heath, after he saw the name of the family friend, Jon Dumont.

As we exited the theater, there they were. Tiffany and Jason, arm in arm. Before I could pull Heath in an opposite getaway course, Tiffany practically side-checked me against the theater door.

In her insistent, nasal tone of voice, Tiffany said, "Jodi, honey! Girlfriend, how funny to bump into you two. Come on, let's all go for ice cream."

This can't be happening. Now Tiffany will spread the rumor that Heath and I am an item. The whole school will be talking about how Tiffany stole Jason from me, and that I took up with Heath right away. I am trying very hard to get over my past Scorpio crush. I don't want to drag Heath into my mess. He is too great a guy to have Tiffany buzzing about him.

On second thought, I am being so ridiculous, worrying about stupid gossip. I am making myself look like a jerk. How about if I go with the flow and see where it takes me? Besides, after eating that globby hamburger with cheese fries for lunch, I needed something to cut the grease, as my father would say. A thick strawberry-banana shake will go down just fine.

"Sure, let's all go to the Good Eats Diner in the food court."

"I know just what I'm going to order," said Heath. "A double scoop of Oreo mint chocolate chip ice cream, with crushed Reese's Pieces, toffee crunch, and fudge toppings. And don't forget the whipped cream," he said proudly of his concoction.

"How icky," said Tiffany. "Just thinking of eating that disaster makes me want to have my stomach pumped."

"Okay, let's go already," said Jason. "I'm starving, and I really want to get my teeth into those great waffles smothered with rocky road ice cream."

Jason, Tiffany, Heath, and I took the escalator to the food court, which was on the third floor of the mall, where all the restaurants were located. We entered the Good Eats Diner and found an empty booth in the back.

Great location, I thought. Hopefully, no one will see us here. I can't believe that I am so chummy with this group. If I had to pick three other people to hang with, it certainly would not be this combination. At least this is a fun restaurant. The theme going on here is the 50s, what with the jukeboxes, pink and blue leather seats, and the poodle-skirted waitresses. It's like we are on the set of *Happy Days*. I half expected the Fonz to walk in and say, "Good job with the screwdriver, Jodi. Is this the little lady that found herself under the table that you rigged to collapse?"

The four of us placed our orders once we were seated. Unknowing observers probably thought we looked liked two cute couples on a double date. Seriously, it was more fun than I had expected it to be.

I used to feel like a Tiffany magnet. I wanted a little space from that stuck-up Tiff and Jason when I was in my Scorpio mode. Now, I don't care whether they are the perfect pretty pair, with his good-looking face and fabulous bod, or her turned-up button nose and drop-dead designer outfits. As a Capricorn, I feel free to take them for who they are. And the good part in this is that Heath can run interference between these two when we bump into each other. After today, it's "see you later, alligator"—or should I say "take a walk off the dock, Kroc"? It's not going to upset me anymore.

When our desserts arrived, we actually started having a normal conversation. We talked about the scary movie, laughed about Ms. Beeker and her detention assignment, and just shot the breeze about everyday happenings. I found myself ignoring the way Tiffany kept punching Jason's shoulder every time he told a joke. I just concentrated on slurping down my delicious shake.

When Mom picked me up later that afternoon, she asked, "So, Jodi, did you accomplish everything on your list?"

"Yes, Mom. And a few things more." If she only knew.

* * *

CHAPTER 19
MY BAT MITZVAH

Today's Horoscope:

Capricorn (December 22–January 19) This year will be a breath of fresh air for you, because the planetary aspects that have been blocking you for so long have finally moved away. Determine what is most and least important to you. Your list may be surprising. Sometimes, the smallest things can mean the most.

"Isn't it funny to be celebrating your birthday in January?" asked Becky.

Yeah, it was so weird on November 18. For the first time in my life, the day was nothing special. No birthday cards, no party. No one said "Happy birthday, Jodi." No checking my yearly horoscope. Nothing.

I am so happy to be finished with my Scorpio days. The horoscopes always turned out to be way off base anyway. It finally all fits together, now that I know my real birthday. And it feels so much better. This year, January 8 was the best!

"And today will be even better," said Mom, as she took me by the hand and led me, Becky, and Seth into the synagogue, where Dad was talking to the rabbi.

"I hope that you aren't nervous, Jodi. You did so well with your Hebrew lessons and bat mitzvah reading practice that it should be a breeze when you read from the Torah this morning," added Rabbi Benjamin.

"Oh, Jodi, you look so beautiful. I can't believe that this day has finally arrived. I am so proud of you," said my father.

"Dad, I have to run to the bathroom one last time before I face everyone. I'll be right back." I ran across the hall to the ladies' room.

Look at me. That's me in the mirror. I am going to be bat mitzvah'd today. I am so excited. I wonder how many of Mom and Dad's family and friends knew of the fake birthday cover-up? And I wonder if the person who actually had the guts to switch my original birth certificate is sitting in the synagogue at this very minute? My parents never really explained all the sneaky details of the switch, and I wouldn't want to be reminded about it today. I don't need any negative vibes when I am standing on the bimah and reading from the Torah.

My thoughts were broken when the rabbi tapped me on the shoulder. "Jodi, it's time to come along and take your seat next to your folks," Rabbi Benjamin said, smiling at me when she found me in the ladies' room.

"Rabbi, I thought that I would be so nervous. So much has happened to me lately. I didn't think I would be ready for this moment, but now that it is finally here, I can't wait to begin."

"Jodi, listen closely. You have gone through a very difficult couple of months, but I am impressed by how you transformed a tricky situation into a positive one. You have bonded with your sister, are more tolerant of Seth, and I can't wait for the congregation to hear about your tzedakah project during your prepared speech." The rabbi escorted me into the sanctuary, where I took my seat between Mom and Dad.

After the beginning prayers and songs, the cantor gave me the cue that it was my turn to walk up the three stairs to join him and the rabbi on the bimah. I remembered seeing some girls and boys tripping up the stairs at their bar and bat mitzvahs, and I didn't want to be one of them now. To prevent myself from stumbling in front of everyone, I raised the skirt of my cream colored dress, which was designed like a lace handkerchief, and daintily took my place at the podium.

As I looked around the room, the sun was shining through the stained glass windows and it lit up the faces of my guests. When I saw their smiles looking up at me, I knew that I was doing a good job with my part of the service. It felt like I was breezing through my readings with very few mistakes, and I took a deep breath before starting my short thank-you speech.

"A few months ago I would have prepared for this day much differently. Of course, I would still have taken my Hebrew lessons with Rabbi Benjamin and studied my Torah portion with Cantor Morgan, but that wouldn't have been enough for me. I would also have pored over my horoscopes, star charts, and maybe even used my Ouija board to plan everything from what I would wear to what I would say in this speech today.

"However, becoming a Bat Mitzvah means that I am on the brink of adolescence and am beginning my journey toward shaping my own individual personality. I have come to realize that I am supposed to question everything, and not blindly follow

the predictions that others have made for me. I now know that I am not only a Capricorn or a Scorpio, but simply Jodi Milner.

"What I know for sure is that I have two wonderful parents who always want the best for me, even if they have a strange way of going about it. And I have a great sister named Becky and a loveable little brother named Seth.

"I learned this lesson from my Torah portion: Charity is the rent we pay for the happiness and privilege we get for our space on this earth. My tzedakah project ties in with this quote, because I have been working with Hands Helping Homeless. This organization builds homes for disadvantaged families. It gives them a decent, affordable place to live.

"Thank you all for sharing this wonderful experience with me and my family."

All of a sudden, a shower of candy was thrown at me from all directions by the guests in the sanctuary, and they sang out "Mazel Tov," which means congratulations.

The doors to the social hall were flung open to reveal a room decorated in jewel tones. Tablecloths of bronze, cranberry, emerald, and amethyst were draped over the large round tables. Huge baskets painted gold were the centerpieces, and they were stuffed with nonperishable foods. Boxes of macaroni and cheese, cans of tuna fish, jars of mayonnaise, juice bottles, granola bars, and various other items were cleverly arranged inside the baskets, which were wrapped in clear plastic. Small tags were tied to the multicolored curled ribbons that were dangling down the sides of the packages. The cards read:

> THESE BASKETS HAVE BEEN ASSEMBLED BY SOME OF JODI'S FRIENDS, ALL OF WHOM ARE VOLUNTEERS FOR HANDS HELPING HOMELESS (HHH). THE ITEMS IN THESE BASKETS HAVE BEEN DONATED BY NEIGHBORHOOD STORE OWNERS AND WILL BE DELIVERED TO LOCAL FOOD BANKS TOMORROW. A LIST OF THESE GENEROUS MERCHANTS IS WRITTEN ON THE BACK OF THIS CARD.

During the cocktail hour, there was a table set up to the side of the room. Its colorful banner was inscribed with the HHH logo and had been painted by some of the children who had moved into the newly renovated homes. Joe Hanlon, my team leader, and his adorable wife, Angie, were manning the table. Joe's wedding band, back on his ring finger, was shining as he handed out leaflets, pledge cards, and volunteer sign-up forms. The guests were three rows deep, trying to take a peek at all the photos of the new homes that the young volunteers had helped to construct.

Other people were standing around the place card table, trying to find where they would be sitting. The cards were shaped like keys, symbolizing the opening of new doors. When I discussed this idea with my parents, I told them that I wanted the keys to represent the doors in the new HHH houses, as well as my own entry into adulthood. I know that this is kind of heavy, but I had given it a lot of thought. After all, I had just turned thirteen, and that's what a bat mitzvah is all about.

When Tiffany picked up her key-shaped place card, she saw a tiny screwdriver drawn on the back. "What does this mean?" she asked Erin. "Do you have one of these?"

"No, I don't have one. Do you, Amber? Marissa?" asked Erin. The three girls didn't dare look Tiffany straight in the eye. They knew exactly what the screwdriver meant, and there was no doubt that I had drawn it.

"We haven't a clue," said Amber. "I guess it means that you are just very special or something."

"Oh, Tiffany, I see you found your place card with the screwdriver on the back. I drew it there myself after we had such a great time at the mall the other day. I wanted to it to mean that we can rebuild our friendship."

Behind Tiffany's back, I saw my three BFF's staring at me in amazement. I would have to explain to them what happened at the mall the other day, and about my new attitude toward Tiffany.

Changing the subject of the conversation, Marissa said, "The room looks so cool. Jodi, I'm so happy that you canceled your original over-the-top zodiac bat mitzvah party."

To think I was going to have a scorpion-themed reception. With my real birthday sign being so messed up, I can only imagine what disasters would have taken place. My party would have made Tiffany's fog machine mess-up and Jason's escaping lizards look like good things. With my luck as a fake Scorpio, crystal balls would have exploded, tea leaves would have dried up, and the palm reader would have broken both of her wrists on the way to the party. I am so glad that I came to my senses.

When the deejay announced the first ladies' choice, I was asked to pick a partner. Jason immediately stood up and started walking toward me, the guest of honor, thinking that I would naturally choose him. I walked right past him as if he were invisible and headed straight in Heath's direction. Heath hadn't even heard the deejay's announcement, and was busy stuffing his face with zucchini and mozzarella sticks, which he was washing down with a chocolate ice cream smoothie. When I tapped him on the shoulder, he was surprised, but didn't hesitate to drop what he was eating and walk with me to the center of the dance floor.

From the corner of my eye I saw Tiffany storm over to Jason and have a hissy fit in his face. "You're always trying to steal the spotlight. Remember, I'm the star. Not you!" she yelled. "Now, let's dance over to Jodi and Heath so we can be seen in the video. We are their new favorite couple, aren't we?"

"Oh, Tiffany. Give it up. You're on your own here," said Jason, as he turned and walked away from her. "I'm going to get something to eat."

Tiffany was left alone on the dance floor, without a partner and with the biggest pout on her face. She looked over at Jodi and Heath, who were really enjoying their dance, and felt even more left out.

* * *

Out of the corner of my eye, I saw the door to the social hall swing open and saw my parents speaking to Ned Biggins. Why is Dad's patient here? This is not the time for a dental emergency. I saw the strange man hand Dad a large white envelope. I was extremely curious about what was going on. Mr. Biggins was not on the guest list. What in the world was he doing here? Even though the dance wasn't over, I excused myself to Heath.

"I'll be right back, Heath. I need a few seconds to see what my parents are up to now. You can never trust those two."

"That man gives me the creeps," I told my parents. "What was he doing at my bat mitzvah?" Mr. Biggins had made a quick exit when he saw me walking in his direction.

"Actually, he brought you a very special present," replied Dad, handing me the white envelope.

I was a little nervous about opening it. Mr. Biggins had trouble written all over him.

"Don't worry, darling. This gift should make you very happy. You have been asking for this for a long time. Go ahead, look inside," said my mother.

I slowly pulled out two official-looking documents. The first one was my original birth certificate, stating that I was born on November 18, 1995. In bold red print, the word "cancelled" was written across the date. The second certificate was almost identical to the first, but instead, it read: born January 8, 1996.

I looked up at my parents faces. "Thanks. This is just what I wanted for my birthday." I slowly ripped the fake birthday certificate into shreds and tossed the scraps high into the air. I hugged my parents, and then ran back to finish my dance with Heath.

After I proudly showed Heath my latest birthday present he said, "I have something to give you, too."

"I am having the best time getting all these presents. What do you have for me?"

Heath reached into the pocket of his suit jacket and pulled out a crinkled old newspaper clipping. "This is an old horoscope that I having been saving, to give to you at the right time."

I slowly unfolded the clipping and noticed that there was no zodiac heading.

> *Jupiter, the planet of good fortune will put you in the right place at the right time. Expect doors to open for you that were previously closed. A romantic partner will be standing right in front of you.*

I looked up from my reading as Heath said, "Here I am, Jodi."

The End

7786939R0

Made in the USA
Lexington, KY
16 December 2010